THE BLACK CHARADE

Dr. Caspian and his wife Bronwen, both possessed of genuine psychic powers, have gained a reputation as investigators of so-called psychic phenomena, exposing a number of fraudulent mediums. They are consulted by prominent politician Joseph Hinde, whose daughter Laura has become strangely withdrawn. He suspects she may be attending séances in an attempt to contact her dead mother. Asked to rescue her from the clutches of evil charlatans, the Caspians' investigations uncover a trail of people dying in strange and horrible circumstances . . .

JOHN BURKE

THE
BLACK
CHARADE

Complete and Unabridged

LINFORD
Leicester

First published in Great Britain

First Linford Edition
published 2014

A catalogue record for this book is available
from the British Library.

ISBN 978–1–4448–1904–5

Published by
F. A. Thorpe (Publishing)
Anstey, Leicestershire

Set by Words & Graphics Ltd.
Anstey, Leicestershire
Printed and bound in Great Britain by
T. J. International Ltd., Padstow, Cornwall

This book is printed on acid-free paper

1

It had to be tonight. The pain and fever had become too intense. Tonight he must go through and be cleansed and renewed, before it was too late.

She had promised. He could wait no longer.

He fought down a cough, clutching a handkerchief to his mouth. The attack bent him double. When he stood up, the crumpled whiteness came away red and foul.

It would be stopped. There would be an end to pain. She had promised.

His fingers trembled as he thrust the pin through his silk cravat. At the last minute she might tell him that the time was still not right. She would torment him, as she had before. There would be some reason, as there had been last time he implored her for speedy release, why it must be postponed. He could not be cheated again. He was ready for the ordeal. If the others were slow they must wait their turn. For himself it had to be now.

He went to the nursery to say goodnight to the three girls. The low flame of the gas jet on the landing caught a glint from one sleepy eye; a tiny, pale hand lay open on the counterpane.

'Goodnight, my loves.'

'Goodnight, Papa.'

His wife came to join him in the doorway, looking uneasily at his face as he turned out of the room. When the door was softly closed she said, in her tightest little voice: 'Henry, you're not thinking of going out this evening?'

'I have an appointment.'

'The fog is settling in. In your present condition it's out of the question for you to leave the house.'

'I must go. I shall be late.'

'What would Dr. McLeod say?'

'Dr. McLeod has said and done nothing to my advantage so far. I shall follow my own course of treatment.'

'And what has *that* advantaged you?' She reached up and turned the gas higher so that she might see him more clearly. 'You should be in bed. Henry, this fog will . . . will . . . '

He knew she had been about to say that it would be the death of him. A commonplace exaggeration but in this case too close to the truth. Death would come if he did not soon take the essential step to conquer both fog and fever.

'I have an appointment,' he said again.

'They'll not expect you in such weather.'

Explanations were useless. Of course he would be expected, whatever the weather. The meetings were governed by signs and calculations far more ancient than the city itself.

He blundered his way past her and went downstairs to put on his overcoat. Even this simple movement clutched at his chest again. He gasped for breath, and another searing cough burned up from within.

'Henry, I insist that you listen to reason.'

Later tonight, and tomorrow, and for all the years to come, she would see her mistake. There would be an end to her whining insistence; a return of the demureness and loving obedience she had shown in the early years of their marriage, before this fiendish thing began to consume his lungs. The pittance from her father and mother, which had kept them going during his illness, had at the same time done them all harm. It was time to set things to rights again. Renewed, he would take his rightful place as head of the household: renewed not in a feeble dream world beyond death but here on earth.

When he opened the front door, writhing wisps of sour yellow fog curled about the antlers of the hallstand. Before his wife could protest again, a hansom turned the corner of the street and sped towards them. He was glad of the excuse to hurry out into the March chill, raising his cane and shouting — a shout which brought another spasm of coughing upon him.

Stepping into the cab and giving the address, he looked back once. Absurd to feel that this was the last glimpse he might ever have of his wife and home.

Absurd, when the truth was just the opposite. After tonight nothing would be changed but himself.

'Gibbet Wharf?' said the cabby dubiously. 'You sure you got the address right, guv'nor?'

'The bridge above Gibbet Wharf, yes.'

'Not much of a place to be strolling round after dark.'

'I can take care of myself, thank you.'

With a light flick of the cabby's whip and a click of the tongue, they were away.

The trim suburban streets ran one into another for ten minutes and more, lit by smears of greenish light on lamp standards almost invisible in the murk. Then even that hazy illumination dimmed. Down some side streets and long terraces there was not the glimmer of a lamp. Occasionally a clear patch opened out, as if some strange ebb had sucked the fog back to the sides of an unsteady square. Once the cabby cursed and tugged his horse to one side to avoid loads of rubble where a new road was being driven through a warren of old houses and alleys. Sputtering oil lamps in a few windows showed

5

that some folk were still clinging doggedly to rooms in buildings, which were being eaten away behind them.

At one junction the glare of naphtha lights picked out the stalls of a street market. Voices drifted like the smell of fish and smoke and vinegar, then died. The cab left them behind and went on into yet darker streets. A fire smouldered beside a pile of scattered bricks, urchins dancing in its glow; then that, too, died.

Henry Garston sat well back, his shoulders jolting comfortably against the padded leather.

They jogged under a railway arch, slowed up a long incline, and stopped at last under the shadow of hunched houses and decrepit sheds.

'Well, this is what you wanted, guv'nor. If you still want it, that is.'

The road humped over a bridge whose iron railing formed also the arch of a low tunnel. Here the dark water of a canal flowed into the open after half a mile underground, still dark until it picked up the reflections of crowded lights on the far side of a wasteland of bricks, splintered wood and broken glass. The red breath of a main line engine pulsed above the long viaduct, the throb and roar of wheels increasing and then slackening as the train slowed towards a terminus beyond the crowded rooftops.

Five years ago there had been a plan to take a spur from that line across the canal and on through north London to new suburbs in the east. A sprawl of slums had been demolished, when the company ran into difficulties and, while waiting to acquire fresh capital, found that more prosperous developers had begun to build smart new estates across their path. The railway line was never completed. Now hills and avenues of tall, fashionable houses bordered a gutted, rusty wilderness.

Garston paid off the cabby, who grunted and drove away.

Lights beckoned across the canal. If he continued over the bridge and up that far slope, he knew how dramatically the streets would change. And he knew that there the little chapel was waiting, tucked away in the gloom, one of the few remnants of what had once been a village set well above and remote from London.

Would the others be waiting there for him, to celebrate his ordeal; or was this evening being offered to himself alone?

He did not cross the bridge but went down the steps to the canal towpath. A dank smell insinuated itself from the tunnel into the fog. He stood on the bank, near the ragged timbers of a wharf, and could just make out a rickety flight of wooden stairs down into the water.

Just as she had told him there would be.

It was all so much darker and colder and fouler than the water in which he had long ago refused to be immersed. He could almost imagine his father and mother, one standing on each side of him at this moment, looking down at that oily flow and asking how he could contemplate such a baptism when he had so contemptuously rejected the white robe and the clean water years ago.

His earnest criticisms they saw as mockery; his honest disbelief a blasphemy. When the boards in the centre of the chapel were taken up and the tiled symbol of Jordan filled with water, all his friends went willingly in to be taken by the minister and dipped below the rippling surface. Such a different surface from this black one before him now. Yet that other one had been unreal. He had not accepted what they told him about it. This one here had to be real. The promises had to be fulfilled. This time he believed.

She had promised.

A great thankfulness caught at his throat, almost as agonizing as one of his coughing bouts. She was there, on the far bank: a more solid shape materialized from the writhings of unstable yellow. He did not speak, but waited, calm now because she was with him. He knew that motionless outline. Even without distinguishing a feature he could tell how she was clad: impenetrably veiled, her cloak hanging sheer and sombre to her toes.

Would she at last show her face when he had reached the far side and been liberated?

She spoke. That unmistakable, hypnotic contralto throbbed across the water.

'How far will you go?'

'As far as is demanded of me.'

'There is no demand. It is for you to offer yourself of your own free will.'

'I offer myself.'

'To the end?'

'To the end.'

'You will not turn back?'

'I shall not turn back.'

'Then come to me now. Come through.'

He went down two steps. The chill gnawed at his ankles. Water plopped in brief agitation against the landing stage. Ludicrously he felt he should be naked, or at least wearing the virginal white shift which would float out on the surface while the minister gripped him and submerged him and raised him again, accepting and accepted.

The rites of that sect had meant nothing. Here was true meaning — through darkness to light, out of pain into wholeness.

Step by step he descended, gasping against the cold. Then there were no more steps. He lurched out into the canal, gasping as this time he gulped noisome water.

He tried to cry out, and swallowed more. His feet were on the bottom but he could not walk. Trailing weed gripped at his feet. He fought free. When his head broke surface he saw the shrouded figure still there, impassive, waiting for him. He floundered towards the far bank. She made no move; simply waited.

He began to cough, swallowed more poisonous water, and coughed all the worse, waved his arms and felt the weed and his own dead weight dragging him down.

He had expected immediate release, immediate cool tranquillity. She had promised. Instead there was black terror.

She was waiting. Of his own free will — that was how he must come to her. If he stopped struggling and abandoned himself to the numbing cold and to all that she had offered him, he would drift to her and be cured. Weakness would damn him utterly. Doubt would be death. He tried to give himself to the slow current and to his faith in her. Water closed over his head again, his feet thrashed in the octopus arms of weed. Lights began to prick and explode before his eyes. He seemed to see the lamps above the baptismal cistern in the chapel of his childhood, and their splashing reflections on the surface. If he had submitted then, perhaps he would never have been visited with illness and never been brought to this.

No. He must not waver. He must be strong enough to reach her.

The bank was within reach. He groped for it, missed, and made a despairing lunge. She must have drawn closer while he was floundering in the centre of the canal. Her feet were just above his head. He reached up with one wavering hand. She stooped and gently touched it, and he felt that now was the moment, now she would draw him out.

Pain lanced through his index finger. It was as if she had clamped pincers or her own incredibly iron fingers on his nail and torn it from him. He cried out, sank, and opened himself to the paralysing water again.

When he rose for the last time he seemed to hear her asking again: 'To the end?' Because there was no hope now but the promised end and what lay beyond, he said: 'To the end.' Now it was only a grotesque bubbling in his lungs, but she would understand. She must understand that he had not faltered.

Her hand was in his hair now.

He would give in. This was the moment. He would close his eyes and miraculously she would draw him out and he would waken on the bank to find that he had honoured the ritual, endured the ordeal, and won through.

There was a last wrench of pain. Surely she had torn a handful of hair from his head?

She had let go, and he was free. Free to sink, and surrender.

⋆　⋆　⋆

She pressed the hank of hair in a cambric handkerchief to squeeze out the worst of the moisture. Then she took the little silver patch-box from the folds of her cloak, coiled the hair into it, and dropped the torn nail on to the coil. The lid clicked shut.

13

She turned and walked back towards the lights of that rising cliff of houses.

At the next meeting the next one must be taken aside and prepared, told that the time was nigh; the next one, so far committed that again there could be no turning back.

2

The chandelier in the coffee room of the Pantheon Club still showed the scars of last November's outrage. Lacking one heavy cluster of drops and pendants, it hung slightly askew. Repairs could have been carried out at the same time as those to the window overlooking Pall Mall, but by tacit consent of all the members this relic of an historic moment had been left as it was, perhaps to remind them that in such revolutionary times they should never lapse into complacency. By the end of this century and well on into the twentieth there would be an accumulation of legends around that unsymmetrical chandelier: colourful fantasies of a night when a peer of the realm had been persuaded to swing from it and thereby bring down a portion in his fall; of a bishop who let a wine goblet fly from his hand in an impassioned appeal to heaven; even of a little-reported earth tremor. In fact the crystal cluster had been demolished by a brick hurled through the window by one of the socialist marchers heading for Trafalgar Square on that bloody November Sunday of 1887.

The Right Honourable Joseph Hinde, Privy Councillor and Secretary of State for Municipal Development in Lord Salisbury's Government, stood staring out of the window as if to raise the alarm should further attacks have to be repelled. A crossing sweeper, brushing steaming dung out of the path of a uniformed colonel on his way to a neighbouring club, caught a stab of the implacable stare and bobbed away round the corner, out of sight.

Viewed from inside the coffee room, Hinde's stance had the air of one turning away in distaste from the two companions at his elbow rather than that of an alert sentry guarding the street. His always austere features were cramped with disapproval. Fellow Members of Parliament might have said there was nothing unusual in this: it was held by many, on both sides of the House, that the length and narrowness of his skull accounted for the narrowness of his opinions and the thinness of his voice. Here in his club, as so often in the House, he could not tear himself away from debate; but suffered by remaining.

'A repeat performance. Invited to amplify the whole subject to the British Association in the autumn. Invited? Ha. Well-nigh commanded. What d'you think of that, Joseph?'

Sir Andrew Thornhill was mightily pleased with himself. His lecture to the Royal Society two evenings ago had been a success: that is to say, it had already stirred up a great deal of argument, which was always one of Thornhill's aims. Hinde's patent disapproval served only to provoke a mischievous pleasure in his restless blue eyes. He was heavier than either of his companions, with broad shoulders swelling beneath the spread of his cheviot coat, and a broad head weighted with a casque of silver hair, his side whiskers seeming to clamp it to his cheeks; but his eagerness and his constant wild gestures made him appear light and feathery, about to fly off across whatever room or platform he was dominating at the time.

'The British Association,' he repeated. 'Hey, Joseph? A pretty contrast, hey, Caspian? There'll be my estimable brother-in-law' — it was as if over the distance between them he were archly nudging an elbow into Hinde's ribs — 'tramping the north giving speeches on traditional morality, whilst I demonstrate that all the old ideas are being constantly transformed into the new.'

'Constantly distorted.' Hinde did not look round, but could not suppress a dour response.

'You weren't even at my lecture, Joseph.'

'We sat late at the House.'

'If you'd heard what I actually said, you would realize there's no question of distortion.'

'What I've heard,' said Hinde, 'was that you've been preaching the possibility of the artificial creation of life.'

'You see? False reports. Overstatement.

I was talking about the prolongation of life. Quite a different thing. And why artificial? If it can be achieved within the natural order of things, then that makes it natural and not artificial, hm?'

Hinde would not be drawn again. He inched nearer the window.

Thornhill tried a wide conspiratorial grin at the third member of the group. 'Don't have to tell you, Caspian. A scientific man yourself. Etheric energy conversion: we all accept now that that's what keeps us going. Energy can't be lost. Can't be created — there, Joseph, how's that for an admission? — but it can't be lost. And it *can* be refashioned. Always being refashioned. Nothing is destroyed, merely changed into another form.' His right hand sketched soaring concepts in the air. 'If matter and energy are indestructible, never suffering anything worse than conversion into another equally vital form, then human life is not a transitory thing.'

Dr. Alexander Caspian said carefully: 'Obviously the race as a race can continue to regenerate itself. The physical matter of our universe will change but cannot dwindle. One accepts that. But the prolongation of individual life . . . no, I'm afraid I have many reservations.'

'Damn it,' Thornhill burst out, 'how can we ever make substantial progress if the best brains in the country are cut off in their prime?'

'We make progress by drawing from what one might call a collective knowledge, amassed over the centuries. Each gifted individual is in fact gifted by his awareness of those sources and his ability to interpret them. The collective progress of the race and its philosophy — '

'Damn collective progress! I want to see things for myself, and to go on contributing to them. Why should a man who has spent so long developing his skills have to give way, often at the height of his powers, to an infant who has to start the whole learning process all over again? If energy itself continues, why should not an existing formation of that energy continue? I'm convinced that the discovery of some regenerative process is waiting, just round the corner, so that those who don't want to be transmuted into other matter may continue in their present shape, with their present faculties. And I want to live to see it. To see how our new knowledge is expanded and perfected.'

Caspian said: 'Such desires are not new. And the knowledge is not new. This all-pervading ether to which you physicists ascribe the behaviour of all natural forces is similar to the Aksashic Record of Hindu mysticism. Paracelsus, too, wrote of just that astral power to which you have given a modern name.'

There was an odd hush. Caspian had half expected a burst of materialistic argument. Instead, Thornhill glanced covertly at him as if wondering what unspoken secrets they shared.

'Perhaps,' said Thornhill with unusual deference, 'the old alchemists knew more than we like to admit.'

'So that's it!' Hinde swung round. 'Gibberish, just as I thought. Pagan superstition. A return to the Dark Ages.'

'I meant merely that if we take those

old concepts symbolically rather than literally, they often turn out to be remarkably close to what we're now discovering by purely scientific experimentation.'

'Such theories are bound to arouse opposition from some of your colleagues,' said Caspian.

'I expect it.' Thornhill was gleeful again. 'I could tell you here and now the names of enemies who'll write scathing denunciations in *Nature*. And a lot of other places.' He glanced past Caspian and raised a hand in greeting. 'Speak of the devil. Or one of them. Old Walton — a bit restive the other evening. I really must go and find out what he made of it.'

He slapped Hinde on the arm and left them, eager for the stimulus of further battle.

Hinde looked grimly at Caspian. 'I was sorry to hear you encouraging his confusions.'

'Confusions?'

'Speaking of ancient charlatans such as Paracelsus in the same breath as modern science. All this Hindu nonsense, too: all the fakirs and fakements being inflicted on us nowadays.' His bleached aquiline features were as unyielding as those of some Old Testament prophet. 'So many of our current social problems derive from such dangerous rubbish. That, to be frank, was what I was hoping to speak about to you. To consult you. Now . . . '

Caspian waited. It would take the man a moment or two to bring himself to confide in a near stranger.

Then it came, hesitantly. 'I am given to understand that you yourself take quite an interest in . . . ah . . . psychic phenomena.'

'In dispelling misconceptions about them, yes.'

'I heard you exposed two fraudulent mediums a month ago. Admirable. Yet the gullible still attend the meetings of these abominable charlatans. People who ought to know better.'

Hinde's lips were bitten in so tightly that they almost disappeared.

After a moment Caspian prompted: 'You have someone particular in mind?'

'I have indeed. I can trust your

discretion, Dr. Caspian?'

'If you have any doubts on that score, better not confide in me.'

Hinde stared full into his face. 'I apologize. I would not have ventured to approach you if I had not heard the highest praise of your methods, from people I respect. And my own judgment tells me I can rely on you.' He cleared his throat, still unsure. 'A glass of wine, sir?'

'When we've finished, perhaps.' It was another gentle nudge.

'Very well. Dr. Caspian, I am a widower. I had one son, killed in the Zulu wars. And I have one daughter, Laura. She is growing strange. I fear she has fallen into evil company.'

'What company?'

'She'll not let me close enough to find out. But when I'm kept late at the House or some official function, I'm convinced she sometimes goes out on mysterious errands of her own.'

'She has an admirer?'

'There would be no need for her to conceal any such. She's of age, it's high time she was married. But she puts men off with that self-sufficiency of hers. Her mother encouraged her to be a bluestocking, and if I become too much the disciplinarian now I fear I'd further estrange her. Since my wife died — '

'Yes,' said Caspian: 'your wife. Couldn't it be that the loss of her mother may have temporarily unsettled the girl?'

'It's more than a year now. And in fact, at first Laura was a great comfort to me. But now she has taken to brooding. Her uncle's influence on her — the way he talks, the meetings he addresses — none of it has been to her good. I wouldn't put it past her' — the words were wrenched from him — 'to attend those infernal séances which are all the fashion, trying to contact the dead. She denies it: but so evasively!'

'You haven't considered following her? Or questioning the servants about her absences?'

'She is of age,' Hinde repeated, 'and she is my daughter. I would neither humiliate her nor demean myself by chattering with servants.'

'But you're prepared to seek my intervention.'

Across the coffee room came a jubilant guffaw from Sir Andrew Thornhill. His voice rose in boisterous argument. With one accord Hinde and Caspian moved into the shelter of the pillared alcove at the end of the room.

'You're acquiring something of a reputation for dealing tactfully with — ah — odd cases,' said Hinde. 'Some way of reading people's thoughts, they say.'

'Do they, indeed?'

'Only metaphorically, of course. Something you doubtless perfected in your career as a stage illusionist. 'Count Caspar', wasn't it?'

'And still is, from time to time. But domesticity has given me a taste for keeping my evenings free nowadays.'

'I envy you. I wish that for me, too . . . ' Hinde broke off. For the first time Caspian caught a glimpse of a vulnerable human being behind that bleak façade.

He said: 'Your daughter may simply be suffering from some extended fit of the vapours. That will either cure itself, or be more appropriately dealt with by a physician than by someone like me.'

'Our family physician finds nothing wrong with her. Such disorders are outside his field. Nor will she confide in him.'

'If we're to meet, it must be done without arousing her suspicion.' Caspian thought for a moment. 'When is your birthday?'

'In October. What has that to do with it?'

'I was hoping Miss Hinde could be persuaded to have her photograph taken as a birthday present to you. But seven months away ... no, that's rather unconvincing.'

'Her own birthday's next week — the 24th of March.'

'Capital. You shall ask her to sit for her portrait as a birthday present from you. My wife runs a photographic studio in South Audley Street. I shall be glad to make an appointment on your daughter's behalf. People are very much off their guard when their picture is being taken, and in the most unobtrusive way we shall find what she has to tell us.'

He had only to think of Bronwen and he was already with her: she was at once so close that here in this male stronghold he felt it would be the easiest thing in the world just to put out his hand and touch her. Across the streets that separated them he seemed to detect the tremor of a response, the loving turn of a head and mind.

'I'm in your hands, Dr. Caspian,' Hinde was saying. 'When shall I bring her?'

'Monday at ten, say?'

'She shall be there. And you'll want me to remain?'

'I should prefer you to occupy yourself elsewhere for at least an hour, and then call back for her.'

'And you'll report to me afterwards?'

'Here or at your home, as you choose.'

Hinde took his arm. 'Now, Doctor, for that glass of wine.'

As they emerged from the alcove and crossed the room, Thornhill flapped an affable hand. Only when they were out of earshot did Hinde quietly confirm: 'Monday morning, then.'

* * *

Laura Hinde stood by the lectern and listlessly turned over the pages of a portrait album, which Bronwen Caspian had opened for her inspection. It was bound in morocco, with gilt lettering on the cover to identify it as the property of The Powys Photographing and Enlarging Studio. Each page of heavy card had a gilt border, framing *cartes-de-visite* of sitters viewed from different angles and with different backgrounds. Some sat stiffly upright and stared vacantly ahead; others stood with one fist gripping the back of a chair. Clients usually arrived with little idea of the pose in which they wished to see themselves immortalized, and it helped to present them with a few samples.

Bronwen edged the mahogany tripod of her camera into position, and through the glass screen established a rough focus on the dais with its lyre-backed chair and potted palm.

'If you care to try sitting beside the small table,' she suggested, 'or standing behind the chair, perhaps leaning forward

— whichever you find most comfortable . . . '

Miss Hinde turned another page. She gave the impression of expecting no comfort.

'I promise it'll be painless.' It was one of Bronwen's stock remarks, usually arousing at least a wan smile.

The girl shrugged and turned towards the low dais. She sat down and folded her hands in her lap. Bronwen smiled encouragingly and rolled a tall cheval-glass on casters round so that the sitter could study herself. For a moment their two heads were caught in the mirror: Bronwen's in the foreground, Laura's remote and elusive, her eyes downcast. Not until some form of registering natural colours was perfected could such a contrast ever be satisfactorily captured. Hand tinting would blur and falsify their two contrasting heads: Bronwen's auburn hair and wide, gently slanting green eyes; Laura Hinde's flaxen tresses bound up too severely for her long, melancholy, beautifully moulded features but still glowing with life in each fine silken strand.

'We'll have to see you more cheerful

than that,' Bronwen persevered. 'I understand this is a present from your father. I'm sure he'd prefer it to be a happy one.'

Laura made an effort. 'You and your husband work together, Mrs. Powys?'

'Mrs. Caspian.'

'I'm sorry. Of course my father told me the name was Caspian, but seeing Powys on that album, and over the studio door . . . '

'It perpetuates my father's name, and my own earlier work with him. My husband indulges me — allows me to carry on the work, and to keep the Powys name alive.'

The girl looked a trifle more animated. 'What a fine thought.' She raised her head, and the touch of a smile showed how ravishingly her features would be transformed if she smiled more readily, more often.

Bronwen stepped forward to indicate how the line of her arm across the pale blue dress would give balance to the picture. A tilt of the head to the left — 'And if you will just let yourself relax, just go slightly back against the chair' — and if only, she thought, she could be sure of catching the essence of that yearning, half-tranced expression. But even her slight intervention had turned the expression sullen and uncommunicative again.

'Let's try a couple of exposures, shall we?' She took a couple of normal poses, then looped some drapery across a screen behind the sitter. 'If you could lean back and look across at the far corner of the window . . . '

She tried to listen to the girl's mind, but sensations were faint. A few shifting images faded and escaped. In her head Laura was as reserved as in her outward manner. But somewhere within the chill defenses of her mind something fluttered: something fearful, like a timid animal peeping out of its burrow and then scuttling back to burrow even deeper.

The sensation intensified. For an instant Bronwen felt herself a hunter, strong and shrewd enough to draw the truth squealing and terrified out of the girl's mind. The awareness was so strong that she knew Alex must be in the building. His mind had joined hers.

She removed a frame from the camera, suggested her sitter might care to consider some of the other poses in the album, and hurried into the darkroom.

He was perched on a high stool in the corner.

Quietly she said: 'You can hear well enough?'

'You know I can. I was with you. Try now. Listen with me.'

They were silent. Across Laura's mind flitted a brief vision of a woman stooping, predatory, her head darkly veiled, two fingers of one hand jabbing an accusation. Then it was gone.

'It's you!' Caspian chuckled. 'The wicked witch of the magic box!' His lips brushed Bronwen's cheek, and he said: 'Do a few more studies, and we'll both concentrate.'

'Are you sure this is right? If she won't confide in her father or their own family doctor, of her own volition, ought we to eavesdrop?'

'She's crying out for help.' His voice was no more than a whisper. At rare moments like this they talked as much with their thoughts as with speech. 'But

33

not knowing what help she seeks. She won't tell all the truth. Even if she did try to confide in the family physician, she would tell him only what she could persuade herself to admit — which has nothing to do with her real ailment. We can't refuse to listen — as much to what she's not saying as to what she is saying.'

Bronwen went back to the studio. The graceful head turned on its long, lovely neck.

'You have some delightful pictures in this album. I'm sure the results of my visit won't compare. Let's not risk any further attempts.'

'Your father's not due for another twenty minutes. We really must do our best for him.' Bronwen moved the camera into a new position. 'Now, can we think of something cheerful? Or someone very dear to you? Or,' she chattered on, 'something that especially interests you? Now,' she said sharply, 'today.'

Caspian's mind was in tune with hers. Both resonated to the conflict in the girl's head. Through the thick mesh of the mental barrier she had erected they got a sudden clear picture of a newspaper advertisement. Then Laura Hinde rejected it again, virtually crumpling it up and hurling it away as if to cancel out anything it had said.

There was a dying whisper of words in that soft tone of hers, although she had not moved her lips.

Yes, I shall be there. To the end. I shall not fail.

The barrier closed again.

Bronwen felt her husband detach himself from her mind. As ever, there was that pang of loss, even though at the moment he was only in the next room.

She took two more plates, and then said: 'There, now.'

A carriage drew up close to the kerb, darkening the long window of the studio. As Mr. Hinde came in from the street, the back door slammed and Alexander Caspian came along the corridor as if newly arrived. The two men shook hands. Laura stepped down from the dais and was introduced.

'Doctor Caspian?' She flinched away from him.

'Of philosophy,' said Bronwen lightly.

Mr. Hinde said: 'A satisfactory sitting, Mrs. Caspian?' His gaze ranged about the walls, and alighted on one of her father's studies of Beaumaris. 'If you should ever want to take pictures of my own establishment for your collection, please do let me know. I think it merits pictorial preservation.'

When father and daughter left, Laura's head was bowed. Bronwen stood in the outer doorway watching. As they reached the carriage she saw Laura glance at Mr. Hinde, apprehensive yet wistful. But when he turned to speak to her she was quite remote and withdrawn again.

★ ★ ★

In the house Caspian had bought on Cheyne Walk immediately after their marriage, Bronwen sat facing him and said: 'The type and setting of that advertisement belong to *The Times*.'

'You plucked that from my mind.'

'I've just identified it, and you caught the gist of what I was thinking. Perfectly normal — for us, that is.'

'And wouldn't it be just as normal for me to think of a thing first, and you to register it?' He laughed affectionately.

She said: 'You're so arrogant.'

But their minds drifted briefly together, and now they were both laughing.

Since the conventional wedding ceremony that followed their mystical union two and a half years ago, when they had pitted their interwoven minds against an engulfing force of evil, they had used their mental powers sparingly. At first the resources of telepathy, which they had so startlingly discovered within themselves were a constant challenge, and a constant shared delight. But the strain began to tell. Too much energy, both psychic and physical, was drained away by too lavish a use of the faculty. It was too precious to be squandered on the conversational exchanges of everyday existence. And what need was there for it, when they could talk and take pleasure in the sound of each other's voices? Bronwen loved her husband's deep, musical, often mocking tone; and loved the movement of his lips when he spoke.

And then, complete surrender of the mind and its deepest secrets to another, no matter how passionately loved that other might be, was too destructive of privacy. Over the years it might even be destructive of the mystery and, paradoxically, the very intimacy of marriage. There were slow, sensual, mutual appreciations more rewarding than too direct an interchange of words or thoughts. Thought transference was for times of stress: a telepathic message was an alarm signal rather than a leisurely comment.

London had added to the stress of using their gift too frequently. First learning its power and their own powers in a secluded Fenland village, they had communicated across the slow-thinking blur of country minds, hearing in the background what amounted only to a passing mumble, a half-formulated notion, with only the occasional harsh spurt of directness — until all those slow minds combined and unleashed a shared terror. The turmoil of the city was different, and dangerous in a different way. Prolonged mental exposure to its millions of unspoken desires and hatreds and confusions brought fierce head-aches and a numbness of the mind: a cacophony of voices dinned unrelentingly in. Attempting to transmit a clear personal message through such discord was like trying to share confidences with a loved one and then having a window thrown wide open, to admit the full clamour of a screaming mob and the crash and screech and jangle of traffic.

Today they had exercised their powers briefly, but still found no neat answer to the question posed by Joseph Hinde.

Caspian settled deeper into his armchair. On the wall behind was Bronwen's favourite picture of him: a portrait photograph which she had superimposed on a painting of a cloaked Mephistophelian figure rising above the Cavern of Mystery in Leicester Square. He had virtually retired from the theatre save for an occasional guest performance, preferring to devote himself to the exposure of fraudulent mediums and magicians rather than the display of his own avowedly, professionally fraudulent magic. Still she cherished the memory of him in his role of Count

Caspar, in exuberant command of his skills and his audience.

Even in this room, at ease in his chair, he exuded the same power. He closed his eyes but thereby became more widely awake. From memory and intuition he sought to call up whatever was relevant to that flash of insight they had experienced.

At last he said: 'No, it's an advertisement we've neither of us seen before. But we recognize certain aspects of it. So I feel it must be in a column adjacent to one of our theatre announcements. Logan will be able to trace it. I'll go round and set him to work first thing in the morning.'

'You can't visualize the exact wording?'

Together they tried to bring the snippet of newspaper into focus from the remembered imprint of Laura Hinde's consciousness. But only a few scattered words survived:

. . . TRUTH . . . death and its banishment . . . Scientific truth open

to all who qualify as mature students
. . . Thursday 12th January.

'At least that date should simplify our quest. We'll most likely find the item during the fortnight or so before the 12th of January.'

★   ★   ★

The full version, when the Cavern of Mystery's advertising manager had tracked it down, sat amid a whole batch of invitations to lectures and meetings: on two successive evenings the enquiring mind in search of self-improvement had a choice between the activities of the Empirical Society, the Paternoster Botanic Club, the Western Hermetic Society, and the Malthusian League, or a free discourse by Madame Helena Blavatsky on The Secret Doctrine. The one that Caspian had been seeking read, in full:

A DISCUSSION GROUP on OUR IN-DESTRUCTIBLE LIFE for discriminating seekers after TRUTH. — Lecture for serious Ladies and Gentlemen worthy of advanced tuition. The illusion of death and its banishment. ETERNITY IN THIS WORLD. Scientific truth open to all who qualify as mature students. Selection meeting Thursday 12th January at The Camden Lecture Rooms N.W.

Bronwen could see and hear it so clearly and depressingly: an hour or more of earnest disquisition in a dank and ill-lit hall, followed by equally earnest argument about Life and Death and the Hereafter and Scientific Proofs of something or other. Every night of the week there were such meetings and such jumbling together of hopes and frustrations all over London. 'But why,' she wondered aloud, 'should Miss Hinde be so disturbed by her memories of that meeting — if in fact she did attend it?'

'I fancy she attended it,' said Caspian, 'but yes, that's our question: what did they teach her that proved so frightening . . . yet so irresistible?'

'She won't have been the only one to

answer that announcement. There must have been others like her, hoping to get something from it.'

'And perhaps, like her, now fearing what they've got.'

3

'Death for you,' said the woman sprawled on the sofa. 'And a sterile life for that creature you leave behind. Unless I take care of her, too.'

'You wouldn't dare touch her.'

'You touched her. You dared. And never came near me again. That's why you'll die, and I'll still be here, watching over her for you. Waiting for her to die too, in her own way, at her own pace.'

First her laugh, then his.

And he said: 'I think you'd better look more carefully at the table, and see where you went wrong.'

Then her scream. Not, thought Elaine Mancroft seven or eight yards away, a particularly convincing scream.

'What have you done to me?'

'It's what you've done to yourself,' said the man by the sofa. 'The poison's in you, Madeleine, not in me.'

Another scream: Really, the poor dear

would have to do better than that on opening night. Elaine stood in the wings and tried to subdue her own agitation by deriding the performance of the two on stage. In a few minutes' time she would show them what power and passion really meant. All their inept fumblings would be overshadowed by her final entrance and the long, vibrant closing speech.

She shivered. She could not stop shivering.

The play had a compelling theme, and a leading part that would have been coveted by any actress. But it had not been fashioned for any actress: it was Elaine Mancroft's, hers and hers alone.

She could not afford to bungle it. Not again; not now, at dress rehearsal.

As she stood in the wings she murmured the closing lines over and over again to herself, a thing she had not had to do for years. The wrong words kept swimming up in her mind. Worse, they kept swimming up in her throat. She tried to swallow, and gagged on them.

Somewhere Adelaide was laughing at her.

She tried to blot out the sound with the sound of those crucial last lines.

'You must make your last entrance very steady,' Daniel had exhorted her. 'It should be doom-laden, implacable. But when you speak you're very quiet. Make them wait for you — and don't say one word until you're at a standstill. Then make it final, despairing . . . beautiful. You can do it, Elaine. If only you'll do it as I've written it.'

He must by now be as scared as she was that she would do it quite another way.

Down there in the stalls he was sitting and waiting for her to make a mistake. Her head echoed not only with his advice but with his barely concealed scorn.

What possessed her?

And what possessed Daniel: did he, in his heart, want her to ruin everything so that he would have an excuse to be done with her? He wanted her to leave, she was sure of it. To go as Adelaide had gone. Or, if not as violently as Adelaide, still to go.

The air whispered with Adelaide's thin, vengeful laugh.

Nonsense. Adelaide was dead. She would never hear Adelaide again.

She heard her cue. 'The lies will have to stop.'

It was impossible to set one foot in front of the other. Out there on stage she would meet Adelaide again: face to face this time, perhaps.

Roderick Grenville glanced over his shoulder. Ten more seconds, and the pause would be too noticeable.

She forced herself forward. But she was moving too quickly. She slowed, and made her way deliberately to the sofa on which the wife of the drama was now crumpled in death.

Grenville turned with a melodramatic start. He had always been one for the grand manner and the violent gesture. Today in the Green Room he had been overpoweringly histrionic even before starting rehearsal: flexing his muscles for the grandiloquence, which his little clique of faithful followers would expect on opening night.

Elaine spoke; and saw the shock in his face.

What had she said wrong?

She tried to grasp the lines and hold them steady. But they were coming out of their own accord and they were not the lines Daniel Clegg had written. Adelaide was taking over. Adelaide was forcing her to say things unrehearsed and unuttered before. She found herself leaning across the sofa, haranguing Grenville and the unresponsive corpse beside him. Her voice was soured by the whining accent she knew to be Adelaide's.

'It's the wrong ending, it wasn't like this, you know it wasn't. The wrong ending . . .'

'We will not say goodbye.' Grenville struggled gamely, absurdly.

'The wrong ending,' she shouted. 'Why are you afraid to write the true one?'

The sofa appeared to be tilting up to meet her. A face swam across her vision and became two faces; three. The back of the sofa caught her across the stomach, and she doubled up over it.

When she was pulled upright it was by Daniel, his fingers biting into her arms.

'What the devil are you playing at?'

'It's too close,' she sobbed.

'Too close? To what?'

'To reality. But not quite. Not honest at the end, is it?'

'What are you raving about?' When she did not reply, because her throat was too choked with fear for any reply, he insisted: 'What is it — what's got into you?'

'Adelaide. Adelaide's got into me.'

He let go of her arms and stepped back.

The other two edged their way uncomfortably yet gloatingly around the sofa. They would have so much to gossip about later. It would all add splendidly to the Clegg-Mancroft legend.

'Adelaide's gone,' said Daniel. 'You know that as well as I do.'

'I know she's waiting for me. Waiting to get into me.'

'Go home. For God's sake — '

'That's where she's waiting now. At home. And she comes at night when you're not there. And on stage she slides her way in between me and my lines, she won't leave me alone.'

'You want everyone to hear you?'

'Everyone will hear you — your version. On stage. In a string of falsifications.'

He tried to steer her across the stage, away from the attentive group in the wings.

'Go home.' he said again.

'I won't let her destroy me. And I won't have you helping her, do you understand?'

'It was a good rehearsal, it was wonderful right to the end. We all get frayed at this stage. When you've slept it off — '

'Sleep is death, and I won't die. I won't, I won't.'

'No, you won't die.' He attempted a laugh. 'You're immortal.'

'You don't care, do you? You've written all your hatred of me, all your real hatred, into — '

'Immortal,' he shouted in a sudden blaze of fury. 'The only sort of immortality you'll ever get — in my plays. Now will you go home?'

She went home.

Mrs. Wraxall heard her arrive, as she invariably did. There was something unnerving in the precision with which that woman timed her tap on the door of the small drawing room, her little nod so un-deferential in its brusqueness, and the setting down of the silver tea tray at Elaine's elbow.

'A trying rehearsal, Miss?'

And always the significant, gently emphasized 'Miss'.

'Very trying.'

'Perhaps you'd care for a small brandy, Miss Mancroft?'

She shook her head. Surely the old harridan wasn't slyly tempting her down the same road, which Adelaide had trodden — towards those steps down which Adelaide had pitched to her death?

Poor lost Adelaide. Nothing to be afraid of. There had been nothing to fear when she was alive, incapable of keeping up with her husband on his ascent to success, such pitiful competition as a woman, and so pitiful in defeat when she had laid her hands — and her lips — on too much gin. So much less to fear now she was gone.

As the door closed behind Mrs. Wraxall, Elaine raised her teacup. 'Rest in peace.' She tried to deliver the line with the brittle offhandedness she would have given to some line from a new Pinero comedy.

Not that she had ever been given the chance of appearing in any of Mr. Pinero's successes. Daniel had long since claimed exclusive rights over her.

Perhaps he was now anxious to relinquish the claim. She began to shiver again. After this afternoon's débacle, what could she be sure of?

Hazily she tried to think herself back into her role, to declaim the lines that had eluded her this afternoon.

'We have shown our honour to be more truly honourable than theirs. But don't you see how she has tainted us? Her disease has run its course. Ours may be just beginning . . . '

All Daniel Clegg's plays had been autobiographical: so much so that it had become a favourite game among those in the know to guess just what domestic conflict he was exposing this time, what bitterness he was squeezing from his system and what scandal might be expected next. Acting his leading roles, as she had done since the year before she moved into his life and then into his bed, Elaine felt herself more and more acting out a cruel parody of the most intimate moments of their life, acting as if in a shop window under the gaze of every prurient passer-by.

This time the story had been twisted to display his own self-justification over Adelaide's death — Adelaide, wife and goad, whose coarse antagonism had inspired some of his best scenes and most telling lines. The character written for Elaine was that of a woman who, watching the man she loved plunge into a disastrous marriage with just such a foul-tongued shrew, stood by him and gave him the courage to fight each battle of his political career, though this meant she had no life of her own and was shunned by society. The climaxes of each scene were provided by the stratagems through which her selfless motives were turned against her by the self-righteous wife, unscrupulously feeding lies to friends and paving the way to a murderous conclusion. In the last act came retribution: attempting to kill her husband, the wife brought about her own death. But Daniel had chosen to end his drama not with a promise of happiness but with a farewell speech in which the woman who had remained faithful through every adversity now renounced the man she loved, denying the hope of any future for the two of them after so much had been contaminated.

Again it nagged at her: was it Daniel's prediction for the future, that she should follow Adelaide out of his life?

Not, surely, the same way as Adelaide, too full of gin, sliding down the steps of the steep terrace on to the crazy paving, which she herself had insisted should be laid there. Food for malicious gossip and speculation; but an accident. It could have been nothing else but an accident.

'You know it's not right.' The flat Midlands voice whined through the faint whistle of the gas fire.

'Leave me alone.'

'Elaine, you know he has cheated on

the ending. Always cheating, our Daniel. Always.'

A shadow curled under the mantelpiece. Elaine tried to out-stare it but lost it in a mist, which ran along the wall and reassembled in a corner, tantalizing the corner of her eye.

'Go back where you came from.'

Back, she thought, to the dank grave and dissolution. To the earth and darkness and the worms. In spite of her resolves and in spite of Mrs. Wraxall she went to the wine cupboard and found the brandy decanter. Burning spirit cut a swathe through the congestion in her throat.

She conjured up a picture of Adelaide's grave, with the earth above it become suddenly transparent, so that she could see Adelaide's thin body swarming with maggots. They ran into unseeing eyes, but the brain hadn't died: it still felt every writhing movement of each and every maggot, taking the flesh to pieces.

Adelaide lay there, knowing that sooner or later Elaine would be dragged down to join her.

'No.' She could not die, she must not. Death would bring her face to face with Adelaide again — for eternity.

She drank, and refilled the glass. The nightmare of Adelaide's vengeance wove itself into her other, most repetitive nightmare: the torment of being buried alive, of trying to struggle out but being weighted down, trapped forever while the mind still went screaming on and on. How can we know we die at once? How can we know the mind isn't immortal, still feeling and understanding everything, but impotent in a decaying body, which at last refuses to answer further commands?

Or a mind strong enough to escape now and then, roaming, disembodied, mocking . . .

'Go back!'

'What was that, Miss?'

Elaine started, and slopped brandy over the rim of her glass.

'Do you have to creep in on me like that?'

Mrs. Wraxall glanced at the level in the decanter. 'Will Mr. Clegg be in for dinner, Miss?'

'I've no idea what Mr. Clegg's plans are.'

Elaine knew suddenly that she, in any event, would not be dining at home. 'I shall be going out,' she said, as much to herself as to the housekeeper. A summons lying dormant in her mind was all at once active.

She must insist on fulfilment of the promise. It must surely be her turn soon, very soon now.

To the end — you will not turn back?

When she was in her bedroom, changing, she said, 'I shall not turn back,' and said it aloud so that Adelaide should be left in no doubt.

★ ★ ★

Laura Hinde was halfway down the staircase when she heard the rustle of wheels on the gravel drive. She stopped, her hand on the banister rail. She was still there, incapable of finishing the descent or of hurrying back upstairs out of sight, when her father came in and slowly took off his silk top hat.

He said flatly: 'I see your gig is waiting outside.'

'Yes, Father.'

'Obviously you were intending to go out this evening.'

'Didn't you say you would be in Stoke for the night?'

'And that is why you made arrangements to slip away to some assignation?'

'Certainly not. It was decided before that.'

'What was decided, Laura?'

'Please, Father. If I don't leave now I shall be late.'

'Late for what?'

She found the courage to continue the descent and tried to pass him in the hall. He stepped back, and his arm barred the doorway.

'Please, Father, you'll make me late.'

'You will tell me what this important assignation is.'

'I can't.'

'You're ashamed.'

'No.'

'Then speak.'

The baize door beside the stairs swung

open, and Sedgwick bustled through. 'I'm so sorry, Mr. Hinde, I didn't hear the carriage. Wasn't expecting you.'

'Quite all right, Sedgwick.' Mr. Hinde let his arm fall to his side, then began to divest himself of his coat. 'Nobody was expecting me.'

His hat and coat were taken away. When the door plopped gently shut again, Laura said: 'Father, I can't keep people waiting.'

'What people?'

'I object to this questioning.'

'Do you, indeed?' It was impossible for her to pass that gaunt, accusing figure. He spoke softly but there was a steely edge to his words. 'For your own sake, my dear, will you not realize that I want only to act in your best interests?'

She stared past him at the door.

He said: 'Please go to your room, and let us talk later.'

'No, I can't. I must go.'

'You will stay here.'

'I can't. I'll die. Do you understand? I shall die.'

'Go to your room. And keep your voice

down. I don't wish the servants to be privy to your hysteria.'

She looked again at the door and tried to make a move towards it. Her father stood unyielding. After a moment her shoulders drooped and she said only: 'I tell you, Father, I shall die.'

★　★　★

The window would need rearranging. These new packages contained some truly enticing volumes, the covers discreet but sufficiently tempting to coax the knowledgeable into the shop to buy. Others would have to be locked away in the back room, ready for special clients who knew exactly what they wanted or who could be persuaded to want things they had not yet contemplated.

A Lexicon of Parisian Diversions, superbly printed and with especially fine plates: Edgar Wentworth turned over a page, and then another. The execution of that arm was very fine; the twisted head and the expression on the girl's face had been caught to perfection.

He turned a further page, studied a few paragraphs of the text, and was tempted to lock the shop door and go upstairs to Annie. But there was work to be done. He must not let his mind wander. With an effort he closed the book and set it on his shelf of items for the connoisseur. He would not sell it for a day or two, though.

The bell over the shop door set up its cracked little clangour. Mr. Wentworth tugged his coat straight, assumed his most pious expression, and went to the counter.

His customer was the same build as himself and probably about the same age, somewhere in the middle fifties. He, too, had the sober mien of a man who deals seriously with serious matters; but his greying beard did not quite conceal the slackness of his plump lower lip.

'Thought I'd drop in on my way to the British Museum. Doing some anthropological studies, you know.'

'Yes, sir. A pleasure to see you again, sir.'

'And what pleasures might you be able to provide today?'

'If you'll wait just a moment, sir. No more than a moment.'

In the back room he lifted from its package one of the new edition of *Choicest Facetiae,* carried it reverently through to the shop, and set it also on the counter. Turning the pages, he stopped casually at a plate that had already caught his fancy.

He had chosen rightly. He could see that from the slight distension of the customer's eyes, the would-be offhanded, man-to-man chuckle.

'Yes. My goodness, yes. Exquisite. Completely free from — uh — vulgarity.'

'Completely.'

Wentworth closed the book. The other man could not take his eyes off the cover as it fell into place. He dabbed at a smear of moisture on his beard, near the corner of his mouth.

'What would you be charging for it, Mr. Wentworth?'

'To you, sir, five guineas.'

'That's a bit steep, isn't it?'

'To a less valued customer than yourself I'd charge more. We're having a lot of troubles. Expensive troubles. Our special consignments from France have been intercepted more than once — terrible loss.'

'Terrible.'

'And when we have translations printed over here, we get some remarkably meddlesome printers. One firm has been known to complain to the authorities. I hear poor Vizetelly's in a spot of bother, for one. Need a lot of care. And that means a lot of money.'

'Disgraceful interference.'

'I couldn't agree more, sir. Why, there's two Members of Parliament talking this very week of tightening up regulations, of closing down shops which offer the cream of intellectual society like yourself the intelligent reading matter it has every right to demand. What do we send these men to Parliament for: to represent us, or to persecute us?'

They shook their heads over the evils of the administration.

'Five pounds, you said?'

'Five guineas, sir.'

A minute later Wentworth was wrapping the volume up.

When his satisfied customer had gone, he turned his attention back to the window. Some titles could be moved to one side to make room for the newer ones.

In the back room, in packing three more French novelties, he let his eyes stray again to the book of plates he had set on the shelf. He turned a page; thought of Annie in such a posture; looked at the clock and saw that twilight was closing in.

Across the courtyard the lamplighter raised his pole. Framed in the entrance of the alley to the Strand, stooping into a pool of light, a boot-black rubbed vigorously at a gentleman's high-buttoned shoes.

Wentworth went to stand in his open doorway for a few contemplative minutes.

He had stood here so many times waiting for Annie to pass with her father's barrow, wanting to be sure of not missing her. Now all he had to do was close the door and make his way upstairs.

He closed the door and bolted it.

Annie leaned, slender and wilting,

against the window frame. She must have heard him opening and then closing the door, and had propped herself there to look dreamily down into the courtyard. She was like a slender young boy, idling as a lad would, gawky and languid and uncommitted. The room was untidy, very much as he had left it this morning but with a torn skirt dropped on a chair and two unwashed teacups added to those already on the table. Tidy in himself and in his household, Edgar Wentworth ought to have reproached her. But one cheeky, gamin smile from her, and he was incapable of anything but gratitude that she should be here.

'You've closed early, aintcher?'

'Got to go out this evening.'

Her face became petulant.

'You're not goin' down *there* again?' The Cockney rasp was shrill and threatening.

'I'm merely going to visit a client with . . . er . . . a valuable collection for sale.'

'Oh, yes?' She mimicked a fierce scowl, which puckered up her little button face. 'Lor, yes, I've heard that one.' She paused, pushed herself upright and ran her hands over her hips. 'I'll give yer the strap if yer late.'

'Yes,' he said happily.

She looked at the large, flat book under his arm. 'You an' yer books.'

He pushed cups to one side, flicking away a few crumbs with his free hand, and put the book on the table. Annie approached as he opened it. From the far side of the table she stared at the engravings upside-down, then edged round to his side, giving off a stale warm smell as warm and animal as that of the trim little donkey she had once accompanied.

'Coo,' she said. 'Fancy them putting that sort of thing in books.' She studied the illustration. 'Well, then. Is that what you fancy?'

He managed a nod.

'Thought you was going out.'

'There's time,' he said hoarsely, 'before I go.'

'And that'll make sure yer don't fancy anyone else while yer gone, eh?'

When they had finished she was

content to lie where she had rolled from him, limbs spread lax and wide on the floor, her mouth still open and murmuring away into silence, while he went to wash. He came back with a clean shirt and dressed by the sitting room fire while she watched him through half-closed eyes, occasionally letting her tongue make a drowsy exploration of her bruised lips.

He adjusted his cuffs. 'Well, I must be off.'

'Mm.' She yawned, and stroked her thigh indifferently.

'Have you had any further thoughts,' he said, 'about going to school?'

She pouted. 'You want to get rid of me?'

'I only want you to be occupied during the day. Some day establishment for young ladies, now — how would that suit?'

She sat up slowly. 'Suits me awright the way things are. What's wrong wiv just bein' here?'

'But what *do* you find to do all day?'

'Just knock about. Could start working me way through them books of yours, I s'pose. That'd be what you might call an education, wouldn't it?'

'Mind you don't get them dirty,' he said fondly.

'I'd say they was pretty dirty already.'

Her laugh followed him and went on ringing in his ears as he left the house. He wanted to stay. But it was for her sake, and for his own love of her, that he was going out. The paradox would have amused her if she had known; and if she had understood.

She had never so much as set foot in a ragged Sunday School. It would take careful education and a lot of application on her part before she could grasp what their life together might be, and what she must contribute.

There was time.

With luck there would be a long, long time. He would be changed and renewed. That was the promise.

He crossed Kemble Court, glancing up once at the lighted window over the shop. She was safely inside, now. Safely lodged where she belonged, instead of crossing the courtyard only at intervals, flitting unpredictably in and out of his life.

She must have come in from one alley and gone out by the other several times before Wentworth noticed her. It was a short cut from the bustle of Covent Garden to the bustle of the Strand, and the costermonger was not going to dawdle here, trying to sell his wares to folk who themselves lived so close to the market: until he found a ready customer in the bookseller.

His daughter must have been about fifteen. Boyish, with a boy's jacket and torn trousers, she aped her father and swaggered like a boy. In rainy weather she wore a cap jammed down on tangled black hair. When it was fine, the hair itself formed a sort of tea-cosy tangle over her head and far down her neck. Once he had noticed her, Wentworth looked for her again. Soon he looked for nothing else. For the first time in his life he was under the spell of a girl.

He did not know why this should have happened to him; but it had happened, and now there was nobody else in the world. He gazed out of the window for hours on end, attending automatically to customers but not daring to look away for too long in case the barrow and the donkey and the man and his daughter should pass and be lost again. When they came in view he would hurry out to buy vegetables from the barrow. If the man served him, the girl would stand back a few paces and give a complacent little grin every few seconds. If she were the one to serve, she would raise dark olive eyes to his face and then lower them provocatively whenever he spoke. Her own face was invariably dirty, but the skin had a darkness that was not mere grime: under her eyes, stains the colour of an over-ripe plum suggested something Italian or maybe Portuguese in her blood. Wentworth found himself stumbling into whimsicalities with her. She answered readily, cheeky and knowing, until her father told her to pipe down; and when Wentworth said he enjoyed it, and such natural charm ought not to be suppressed, the father regarded him suspiciously and the girl with full understanding.

Then she stopped coming.

The first time, he found he could not ask where she was. There was something too surly in the coster's attitude. But the third time, aching for news of her, he asked as casually as possible: 'What's happened to your little helper? Haven't seen her with you recently.'

'Not much of a helper, she wasn't. Except,' said the coster meaningly, 'in attracting customers, you might say.'

'She found the work too arduous?'

'She found herself a reg'lar. Settled in with her own feller. Got themselves a room down Clerkenwell. Let's see what 'e can make of 'er. Fancies his chances at moving off the barrers and settin' up as a greengrocer somewheres. And he ain't got himself a decent pony and trap, let alone a shop. Finish up in a dosshouse, both of 'em, I wouldn't be surprised.'

'Couldn't you have stopped it?'

'Suits me. Makes a bit more room at home.'

'They'll get married?'

The coster spluttered a wide guffaw. 'Married? No guilt in getting' married.

71

Leastways, not as I've ever heard tell.'

Alone, Wentworth paced in memory the streets of Clerkenwell. It would not be too far a drive from the hall of the Young Men's Self-Improvement Association where he lectured. But of course he wasn't going to be such a fool as to go there. A fine fool, at his age. He'd probably get mauled, as he had been on one occasion in those parts after walking home with a boy from his lecture class. It was unseemly to want so desperately that slip of a girl because she looked like a boy; but not like a boy. He would forget her.

He did not forget her. On the evening of his next talk to the society he gave them less than their usual quota of his time and escaped into the streets. He recollected the name on the barrow — Tucker — and asked about the family from a chair-mender in one street, a shellfish seller on the corner of another. And about the girl in particular. He made it sound as casual as he could, but encountered some odd looks and backed away and went home, though not to sleep.

It took two weeks to find her, and by

then it was no use telling himself that tomorrow or the next day he would abandon the humiliating chase.

Finally he came to her in a room, which could be reached only by squeezing past three beds and a landing window draped with sacking. The building had once had a central yard, now obliterated by a piling up of sheds and lean-to's.

She showed no surprise at his arrival. She was even grimier, her hair even more matted, than when he had last joked with her. But the wicked sparkle was still in her eyes, and she was immediately on her feet and moving towards him with just the faintest twitch of her hips.

'I intend to take you away from this place,' he said.

The girl said: 'Not until *he* gets back.'

''Perhaps it would be better if we just — '

'No,' she said. 'It wouldn't be better. Not bloody likely it wouldn't.' She grinned, very close to him. 'Don't worry, he's only gone round the corner. He'll be back in five minutes.'

Wentworth was sure that he had done

one of the maddest and riskiest things in his life. But he could not have called off the pursuit.

The lad came back. He had large hands, which clenched when he set eyes on Wentworth and remained clenched as Wentworth tried to find a way of saying that he wanted to take the girl away and give her a good home. He had expected questions — what sort of a home, what would she be expected to do when she got there, what was all this leading up to? — or outright curses. But the lad kept his scowling gaze fixed on the floor, and asked only one question at last: ' 'ow much?'

'What do you mean?'

'You can 'ave 'er for ten quid.'

'Disgraceful.'

'Seven, then. Call it seven. But not a penny less.'

His eyes widened when Wentworth took out a five-pound note and crackled it between his fingers.

'Not a penny more,' said Wentworth.

It was all done within two or three minutes.

As they shuffled along the landing past

the beds and down the rickety stairs, out across the noisome yard and at last into the street, Wentworth asked: 'What's your name, child?'

'Annie, sir.'

'Annie Tucker.'

'Not rightly, mister. Used to be Annie Johnson, but my mum shifted abaht a bit, so I don't know if it still is.'

'Never mind. Annie will do.'

One person for whom Annie, however, would not do was his housekeeper. Mrs. Burnett had primly and uncommunicatively kept the rooms above and behind the shop tidy this ten years, herself sleeping in the tiniest attic of all under the roof at the back. She gave no sign of disapproving, or indeed of having any opinion whatsoever, of his stock in trade; and if from time to time he brought some young boy home for a night or two she was invisible and inaudible. But somehow a girl like Annie would not do. When she left, she brought herself to say: 'Well, I only hope that young lady can look after you as well as I've done. I only hope so, that I do.'

Meaning, thought Wentworth with amusement rather than resentment, that she hoped just the opposite.

In fact if there was any dusting and tidying and making of beds to be done, he found he had to do it himself. It was not that Annie was unwilling: when he suggested that with so much time on her hands she would surely be happier making herself useful about the house, she smiled and said yes, that was all right, she'd do her best and glad of it; but when he came up from the shop he would usually find her squatting in the middle of the floor, sometimes with the morning paper or a few magazines crumpled beneath her, heedless of the litter she had created.

He had managed well enough before Mrs. Burnett came on the scene, he could manage now that she had gone. What he could not have managed now was to live without Annie.

'Mind yer not late, now. I've warned yer.'

She had pushed up the window over the shop and was leaning out, ghostly and tempting in the dusk. He waved, not trusting himself to answer, and walked away.

He had spent so many dull years, depressing and often shameful. Now he had something to live for.

Perhaps this very evening it would be his turn to be beckoned on to the next stage.

*　　*　　*

'So,' concluded Sir Andrew Thornhill, 'in a world which is daily yielding up more of its secrets and fitting old beliefs into new contexts, in which ancient and supposedly dead organisms produce the fuels to warm our life and drive our engines, in which medicine shows man's dependence on the products of the earth and of the very air, in which so-called discoveries prove frequently to be only a revaluation of matters with which our forebears were perfectly familiar under less scientific names, we must increasingly turn our attention to the relationship between apparently inanimate matter and our own life forces.

'What some would superstitiously cling to — or, at the other extreme, contemptuously dismiss — as sympathetic magic may, after all, be revealed as a valid scientific relationship whose further exploration will make possible the development of powers which man has hitherto misinterpreted and feared to investigate. This is not mysticism: it is the logical extension of the natural sciences.'

He allowed twenty minutes for questions but replied with less than his usual expansiveness. His mind was already reaching on ahead.

Anticipation mounted as he approached the chapel in its quiet street, a dark shape set back from its neighbours so that no light fell on it. Each time he arrived he was surprised by its existence, and surprised that he of all people should be entering such a place. Somehow it ceased to exist between visits, and if asked about it in the middle of an otherwise ordinary conversation he would not have been able to recollect what place was being referred to, or where it could be found. But now, just for an evening, it was the only reality.

He went up the chipped, tiled path and pushed the door open.

Inside, the darkness was leavened only by feeble light from an oblong sooty window beyond the pulpit. He paced up the aisle. On either side the old horse-box pews were stacked with shrouded objects, some reaching halfway to the rafters. Only the front few ranks of pews remained uncluttered. He stood with his hand on the latch of the one he had been assigned, the top of the door coming to his shoulder. His eyes were growing accustomed to the gloom. Yes, there was the expected shape in the pulpit: the outline of a veiled head.

'You are the first,' she said.

It was an opportunity for speaking his mind to her, without challenging her authority in front of the others.

'Do we really have to sit in the dark all the time? Why can't we sit and talk in normal conditions, seeing one another, sharing our experiences and working things out between us?'

'Because, for what we are exploring, the dark is a normal condition. Our procedure will function only in accordance with its own specific laws.'

'I can't see why a little light on the scene would impede it.'

'If you find that some experiments work only in the presence of water, and others in a vacuum, you don't insist on testing them over and over again in the wrong conditions — except to prove that they are the wrong conditions. The phenomena we seek will not flourish in the glare of daylight for anyone to see.'

She was, he realized, soothing him with his own kind of terminology. There was nothing to do but accept.

Respectfully he said: 'When do I move on to the more advanced studies . . . to the transformation itself?'

'Your time will come.'

'This long drawn-out procedure — '

'Again, you must consider it in your own scientific idiom. Certain chemical reactions require certain times and temperatures. Hurry or delay the process, and it is ruined. So with us.'

' 'Us',' he echoed. 'Somehow I get the impression that the others aren't in the same mould — I'm not sure we belong together.'

'I assure you that you're all part of one pattern. You must all partake in the same rituals. You may not understand the necessity for this, but for century upon century it has been proved to work.'

Thornhill laughed. The sound ran away into the dusty recesses of the chapel. Again the woman had struck the right, shrewd note for him. He felt she had invited him closer, acknowledging in spite of what she had said that he was distinct and apart from the others in the group.

All at once she said: 'Are you beginning to doubt?'

'No,' he said hastily. 'No, I wouldn't want you to think that.'

'You'll not turn back?'

'I'll not turn back.'

Behind him the door creaked. He stepped into his pew and sat down. Footsteps came up the aisle and moved into the pew immediately below the pulpit. The steps had been those of a woman. Then came another — and was that the sound of a third?

There was silence.

Thornhill counted. One fewer than last time — or was it two? One of course had moved on since last time: the fortunate, chosen one who had gone ahead. But still they were short.

Something was wrong.

The silhouette in the pulpit was as motionless as if it had been carved from the woodwork.

At last she spoke. 'Someone is missing. One has failed us.'

Thornhill cursed silently. Behind him a woman let out a pitiful little moan.

'One has turned back.' The voice from the pulpit was steady, but thrummed with a fearsome condemnation. 'We shall have to recall her. Or eliminate her from our calculations — cancel her out.'

4

Joseph Hinde said: 'If I didn't know it to be absurd I'd say she was willing herself to die.'

'Why should it be absurd?' asked Caspian quietly.

'We're in England, sir. Not in some fetish-ridden backwater of barbarism, under the spell of some black sorcerer.'

'We are all subject to the sorcery of our own fears.'

'It's stubbornness. Sheer wilfulness on her part.'

'Even if that is so, if what she's willing is her own death she might all too easily achieve it.'

They sat in Hinde's drawing room, its semi-circular construction emphasized by the sweep of bay window looking out on the garden and the River Thames beyond. In the ceiling, moulded medallions framed the chaste, blind-eyed faces of classical goddesses; and in the wall facing

Bronwen was a tall niche accommodating a marble nymph with downcast gaze.

The pose bore a striking resemblance to that adopted by Laura Hinde in one of the photographs lying on the marquetry table between Mr. Hinde and Bronwen. Her eyes strayed to it, and once again she envied the exquisite line of the girl's neck and her fine cheekbones.

Caspian said: 'She has seen a doctor, naturally?'

'Naturally. I've had our own man in every day, and got Grisdale out here from Wimpole Street.'

'And their diagnosis?'

'The usual talk about vapours, and fugues, and nervous depressions and a touch of anaemia — and of course it will all be cured of its own accord once she is married. So we must find the girl a husband. And in the meantime Grisdale recommends taking the air at Bognor for a few weeks. Fresh air? It's all I can do to get her to walk in the garden, and that brings her nigh to collapse.'

Caspian rose and walked into the arc of the window, staring thoughtfully out. Past him. Bronwen could see the distant Corinthian pillars of the gates on the Chiswick road, and one edge of a little classical temple on a knoll. The river gleamed decorously in its well-proportioned, well-disciplined curve. Outside and in, the contours of Nasmyth Lodge were coolly and formally composed. Flowerbeds had a mathematical correctness, and the hedges were clipped like a military haircut, with no hint of topiaristic fantasy.

Hinde picked up one of the studies of his daughter and contemplated it glumly.

'An excellent likeness. But the expression is disturbing. One sees the beginnings of the malady already, wouldn't you say?'

'It was a deliberately meditative pose,' said Bronwen. 'I wouldn't read too much into a posed photograph.'

'But she came to you to be read, as it were. The photography was merely a pretext. And now where are we?'

Over his shoulder Caspian said: 'What we read was an invitation to what appeared to be a discussion group. It had come to mean a great deal to her, but for some reason she was afraid to divulge its full significance.'

'You asked her?'

'In our own way, yes.'

'You see!' Hinde, too, rose to his feet. With his back to the silvered mirror and carved vine tendrils of the large overmantel, he instinctively raised his right hand to his lapel. He might have been in the House, preparing to demolish an opponent. 'These pestilential societies, undermining the nation. Disguising their pretensions with even more pretentious names — and concealing heaven knows what depraved practices in their sordid meeting places.' His sonorous tone was less ill-tempered than his actual words. 'I shall shortly present the House with a motion calling for a Select Committee to enquire into the spread of obscene publications and the worse obscenity of pagan practices seeping into the British bloodstream: evils of the spirit, and evils of the flesh.'

'Much of it,' said Caspian, 'a revolt against the impersonality of mechanical progress and scientific determinism.'

Hinde's face closed austerely against this.

Bronwen signalled a demand to her

86

husband's mind. When she felt his answering awareness she said silently across the room: *Ought we not to be dealing with Laura instead of playing with generalizations?*

Caspian acknowledged the message with a slight nod. To Hinde he said: 'Do you think Miss Hinde would agree to see me?'

'She'll neither agree nor disagree. She lets things happen around her as if none of them could conceivably be any concern of hers.'

Hinde reached for the bell pull, and when the butler appeared asked for his daughter's nurse to be brought down. While they waited, Caspian said: 'With your permission I'll attempt to mesmerize Miss Hinde.'

'I confess I fail to understand your methods, Dr. Caspian,' Hinde said uneasily.

'I'm not surprised,' said Caspian blandly. After a moment he added: 'We shall need to be left alone with her — my wife and I.'

The nurse was a respectful but

sceptical-looking woman who took her employer's instructions without conveying any suggestion of professional agreement or disagreement. She showed Caspian and Bronwen up to an attractive little boudoir with the lightest lavender-tinted curtains. Laura lay on a chaise-longue against the wall farthest from the window, her head turned away from the thin afternoon sunlight. One arm was draped over a cushion. Her slender fingers hung above a small hump of colour on the low table beside her. Making no sudden movement, Caspian picked it up. It was a millefiori paperweight, glinting with a dozen colours as he turned it slowly to catch what light there was. Bronwen saw a spark of crimson from a central floret; and saw Laura's head turn as if to follow the gleam.

'It was her mother's,' the nurse confided in an undertone. 'So Mr. Hinde tells me. She sets great store by it.' The curls of her mouth indicated that she was used to the fads and fancies of children large and small. 'I'll be along the landing,' she said, 'two doors along, if you want me.'

Bronwen remained near the door. Laura gave no indication of noticing her or of connecting her in any way with the man now drawing a cane chair close to the chaise-longue.

He turned the paperweight so that it shone faintly into the girl's eyes, then rocked it to and fro, a fraction of an inch either way, steady and gentle. After a full minute he said quietly: 'It brings back memories, Laura.'

Her lashes scarcely blinked.

'Memories,' he intoned, 'of what you love best and want most. Of what you see in dreams. What is being talked of in your dreams, Laura?'

The girl leaned more heavily on the elbow-rest but there was no sign of her eyes glazing into a trance.

'Your friends are around you. You're learning from them. Can you share what you've learnt?'

Laura neither protested nor yielded. She watched the glimmer of light come and go but her mind reflected nothing. Still Caspian went on: an interminable four minutes, five minutes, on and on, murmuring, coaxing. When a picture did at last begin to form, Bronwen felt it was a whim of Laura's rather than an answer. None of them was looking out of the window yet they shared a vision of the entrance gates, far away down the drive, closing. Closing forever, and in some way not shutting Laura in but shutting her out. Forever.

Despair and yearning were too great for speech. Then through the swell of that despair Bronwen and Caspian glimpsed another brief picture. A veiled woman leaned forward into Laura's mind as if to answer her call. Not, after all, the identification with Bronwen herself which they had misread on that occasion in the studio, but a hooded predator with two clawed fingers jabbing forward in condemnation.

Laura's lips moved. 'No. Oh, no.'

Her mind was no longer blank. Stillness was lashed suddenly into a storm. Bronwen and Caspian shook beneath the blast: spray blinding them and shrieking about their ears, and the undertow dragging shifting sands from beneath their feet.

You have betrayed us.

'No.'

You are rejecting me. It was a woman's voice, a woman's thought — but somehow not in Laura's accents.

I don't want . . . I mustn't . . . Laura faltered. Another wave of despair rose and fell away.

But you do want. As I want you.

The surface was reduced to a steady swell, the breakers subsiding into slow, seductive undulations. Laura's head moved to follow alternate beats of the paperweight's gleam.

I shall be with you — a susurration like the tug of ripples on shingle. Laura shook her head a fraction more quickly, then opened her mouth to breathe a wordless prayer.

The fingers reached for her again. They were no longer accusing talons but soft and white: two hands and two bare arms reaching to encircle Laura's body. She moaned sweetly. Bronwen no longer sensed the touch of clothes, of a silken grip at wrists and throat, a skirt's weight on the knees. Instead there was nakedness: flesh caressed flesh, teased, and moulded itself against yielding softness. Lips touched and parted. A kiss was dabbed on the left breast, a hand moved in shameless insistence. Woman to woman, two bodies clung together and arms entwined, desperate to touch and know all. A swooping kiss drew a gasp from Laura, her mouth open and trembling, her whole body opening and pleading.

I am Ilona.

Yes, oh, yes.

Return and you shall be with me.

Forever. You promised.

Arms tightened on her. Sweat ran between her shoulder blades.

Return and ask forgiveness.

The two bodies dissolved into each other. Laura cried out in ecstasy, yet at the same time fear and revulsion were struggling to the surface.

You are rejecting me. The accusation came again, and instantly Laura's nakedness was left cold and alone.

No. Come back, please . . .

Lilith I was, and Salome. Elizabeth and

Lucrezia and Theodora. The syllables were a lullaby, a crooning music rather than names. *And Ilona.*

Laura's mind cried: *I shall be Ilona.*

No, this time it will be different. This time, and the next time, and the times after that. Together we shall know . . .

Bronwen felt that she was losing her balance and falling forward. She reached out to hold on to Caspian, and aloud she said: 'Who is it? Who are we listening to?'

The deep revulsion that had been struggling up through Laura's inner fever was at once released. It swept across their minds and wiped them clean of the sensual, caressing incantations. Laura whimpered. Her body ached, she groped out with one shaky hand and then, as the fabric of her sleeve rustled against her arm, fear and desire drained away and the outlines of the real world solidified about her.

Caspian put the paperweight back on the table. Laura let her hand stroke it a couple of times. The base was warm from Caspian's palm, but the upper surface was cool and uncommunicative.

Her eyes met Caspian's. 'What happened?'

'You don't remember?'

'No. Only . . . ' An echo of that sense of loss disturbed her briefly, but meant nothing she could define. She said: 'Nothing.'

They told the nurse they had finished, and went downstairs. Halfway down, Bronwen said: 'I'm sorry. It was my fault that the thread snapped.'

'I don't think she could have gone on much longer. She was under great pressure.'

'From whom? Who were we listening to?' Bronwen asked once more.

'To Laura.'

'No, there was someone distinct from Laura. You heard that as clearly as I did.'

'Distinct from Laura as we know her. Which is not very well, so far. We have no idea what fantasies she creates for herself; or has been helped by others to create.'

'D'you suppose she's been dabbling in a witch cult?'

'Whatever it is, the group probably laid down its own code of secrecy, fraught with penalties. That's something all these societies have in common: for most members, part of the pleasure lies in the feeling that one belongs to something special and privileged, spiced with a little danger. Masons, would-be adepts, suburban wizards, all have their pathetic little secret vows, backed up by dire threats if anyone should reveal those secrets to outsiders.'

'Only symbolic nowadays, surely?'

'If a man believes, as African natives believe, that when a witch-doctor points a bone at him he will waste away and die, then he — or she — will waste away and die.'

'And that woman, enticing the girl and then accusing . . . '

Their voices had attracted Hinde's attention. He appeared in the hall below them, at the foot of the stairs.

'Well, Dr. Caspian?'

They went down to meet him. 'Miss Hinde said very little,' Caspian hedged. 'One can't always guarantee cut-and-dried answers from mesmerism when the subject has an innate reluctance to be mesmerized.'

Hinde looked pleased rather than disappointed. He was probably telling himself that of course no child of his would subject herself to such nonsense.

'Nevertheless,' Caspian went on, 'we're more than ever convinced that she has been associating with some group which has made a disturbing impression on her mind. Eradicating that influence will be difficult without her full consent.'

'So those powers of yours that I've heard so much about aren't up to this kind of thing?'

'There are no ready-made cures and no ready-made miracles. For a time I propose to concentrate on routine investigation. When we've grasped something of the motives of the society she's been involved with, we may have a clearer idea of her own motives.'

'I hadn't envisaged your proceeding as a mere private enquiry agent.'

'You mistrust anything which smacks of homeopathic methods,' said Caspian, with the first snap of rancour he had allowed Hinde to provoke: 'of attempting to cure like with like — psychical problems with

96

psychical antidote. And when I propose to make more mundane enquiries, you're equally mistrustful.'

Hinde flushed, not with the usual red seeping through his features but with a disquieting blue sclerotic stain which glowed up to the height of his cheeks and hung there a few seconds before burning slowly away.

'Of course you must do what you think best, Dr. Caspian. I have placed my daughter in your hands. I must leave her there for as long as you honestly feel there is a chance of making progress.'

As he led them out under the portico, Hinde glanced up at his daughter's window. 'There's one thing to be thankful for. At least while she's here at home she's safe from any further damage from those evil-doers, whoever they may be.'

Bronwen and Caspian shared the unspoken doubt: *Is she?*

* * *

A polite approach to *The Times* earned an indignant rebuff. The clerk in the advertisement office made it haughtily clear that it was not their policy to divulge names and addresses of those who entrusted their wants and announcements to the columns of the newspaper. If the gentleman cared to send a letter care of the paper it might, however, be forwarded to the appropriate party.

'Are we going to write?' asked Bronwen.

'Whichever way we framed the letter it might put our quarry on the alert. At best we'd get no reply whatsoever. At worst someone might start investigations in our direction and so discover our connection with Miss Hinde.'

'I'm still worried about that 'someone'. She might already have discovered our connection. She was there with Laura: an actual part of Laura.'

'Part of the girl's self-created fantasy.' Caspian picked up his earlier train of thought.

'Nothing more, then, than some inner mental disturbance? No influence at all from outside?'

'Let's not misinterpret the symptoms.

When a patient's out of sorts, her doctor should first try to establish whether she has indigestion or a passing megrim before operating for a tumour or committing her to a madhouse.'

Bronwen permitted herself a secret smile. Always her cherished, stubborn Alexander would strive to remain a sceptic, construing nothing in supernatural terms until he had been forced to discard all natural hypotheses. It was one of his strengths and had saved them from pursuing many a misleading trail of superstition. But another of his strengths lay in reserve, waiting to be summoned when all everyday explanations had been eliminated and it was necessary to confront those things, which went beyond reason.

This time she hoped his matter-of-factness was justified. Let there be a conventional medical explanation. But her own intuition, as stubborn as his rationalism, made her a devil's advocate.

'What sort of vapours could bring on such cravings in a girl of that upbringing?' Absurdly she felt shy of her own husband, of having shared those carnal perversities with him and with Laura — and with that other.

He responded with a slow, loving smile. 'Don't you see the parallel between the ritual patterns she has retained from those secret meetings and her own sense of deprivation? Her subconscious mind interpreted the group's philosophies in the light of her own fears and loss. Her mother's death was a numbing blow. Seeking some answer to fate's cruelty — '

'She reacted against her father?'

'Not against him as a person, I think. She's fond of him, but they have difficulty in communicating with each other. What she shies away from is his assumption that, like every other eligible girl of her age, she ought to take herself off his hands by putting herself up for auction among the marriageable young men within their social circle. Not being ready for that, and still bruised by her mother's death, she retreats into obsessive fantasies, communing with a chimera of her own creation.'

'Sappho. That was one of the names

running through her mind.'

'And her body,' said Caspian quietly. 'It was the dream of Lesbos and its practices which inflamed her. But at the same time she was appalled by those flames. Appalled by the heat of her own response. She's scared of what she has revealed about herself: revealed, above all, to herself. Perhaps that's the whole answer.'

'So you won't bother following up the society after all?'

'Of course I shall follow it up. We need to know just why it should have been able to affect her in such a way; and whether she can be cured simply by our exposing its mediocrity.'

⋆   ⋆   ⋆

He went to inspect the Camden Lecture Rooms.

What might almost have been two small schoolrooms, each with an iron stove in the centre of the floor, flanked a hall with a low platform on which stood a table covered by a puce chenille cloth. The caretaker showed Caspian the premises and, assuming that he wished to make a booking, directed him to a Mr. Noakes, some ten minutes' walk away. Mr. Noakes confirmed that he was a trustee of the hall, and yes, he was responsible for accepting bookings and payment for use of the premises. But no, he didn't keep very detailed records. As long as the money balanced that was good enough. He had his own job to do, times were hard, and there were only twenty-four hours in a day. No call to make entries of every group that used the place. All sorts of crackbrains and cranks met there, and the trustees had no objection to any of them so long as they paid up and caused no trouble. Not that there ever was any trouble.

'Got perfect faith in Emery. Can safely leave him to keep an eye on things, clean up, and close up.'

'Emery would be the caretaker?'

'Never a thing to worry about, with Emery in the building.'

Caspian went back to the caretaker. With some prompting the man did recollect, 'Now you mention it,' one lot of folk around the middle of January who'd gone on about some sort of life force and a new rhythm you had to learn before you could live properly. 'Only caught a few snatches here and there, you'll understand, when I was waiting to sweep up.' Would they be the ones, then — the ones who dressed up in white robes and hung the place with mistletoe?

Caspian thought not.

'Well, then.' Emery pondered. 'Or the one round about the same time, with the lady who always wore a veil — or more like a hood, pretty well right over her head?'

Caspian thought of two pictures, the one blurred and misleading, the other clear and menacing. Slowly he nodded.

'A funny one, that one.' Emery was pleased with his own feat of memory. 'At least you have to say it of that Madame Blavatsky: she don't mind showing her face. Something creepy about that other one.'

'Did you hear any of *their* proceedings?'

'They didn't like me hanging about when they'd settled in.' He accepted the sovereign Caspian was offering. 'You get all kinds. These was what you might call a nobby lot — very respectable, you know the sort I mean. Not many of them, mind; and a sight less at the second meeting a week later. Only they'd thinned out by then, and I'd say not making much progress.'

'Any further meetings?'

'Not here. Often happens like that: a lot of talk at the start, and they're all going to alter the world one way or another, and then attendance drops off and it all fizzles out.' The caretaker evidently felt that after being so obliging he was entitled to a few confidences in return: 'You wanting to get in touch with them, find out if they're still going? You weren't one of the original lot, so far's I recall?'

'I'm anxious to find someone I've lost contact with.'

'Like I said, you get all kinds.'

Caspian said: 'The woman with the hood — did you talk to her at all, perhaps after the end of the meeting, when she was getting ready to leave?'

'She was always the first to go. In a

hurry, as if she didn't want a word from anyone. Not even a goodnight. You know, like an actress who can't be bothered with stage-door johnnies and just wants to get home. But there, now!' Emery burst out suddenly. 'I'd swear I knew one of the others, because it struck me as funny seeing the likes of her in a place like this. Not right for her, and her not up on the stage herself running the show.' He savoured his dramatic moment. 'Elaine Mancroft.'

'The actress?'

'As sure as I'm standing here. Swear it, I would. That voice — there can't be two like it, can there?'

'It's unlikely,' Caspian agreed.

'And going out, I got a bit of a look at her, and I'd say it was her all right. Not that I've seen her that often, and then only from a long way back in the theatre. When I get the chance it's more likely to be Collins's, a bit of good music-hall, that's more my fancy. Or a night out at the Cavern of Mystery — now, that Count Caspar, that's what you might call a performance.' Emery looked into

Caspian's face for agreement, then let out a long low whistle. 'Just a tick, now. It's over a year since I saw you . . . but it is you, isn't it?'

Before Caspian could decide on something suitably non-committal, the caretaker went on: 'You can't tell me it's not. And I've heard about those other things you get up to — chasing after mediums and that lot. Look, sir, we don't hold anything against folk who hire this hall.'

'I didn't for a moment suppose — '

'Provided they pay, and conduct themselves proper, we don't make ourselves a nuisance. I don't think Mr. Noakes would like anyone starting up any unpleasantness.'

'I assure you I have no intention of starting up any unpleasantness.'

'Yes, well. I think I've told you all I know, sir.' Emery backed away to the entrance, ran a finger over the brass door handle, and examined it. 'Better be getting on with my work.' He was holding the door open. But as Caspian went through, Emery added: 'I'll say one thing, Count — watching you magicking everything the way you do, I don't see why you don't just snap your fingers and conjure up whoever you're looking for, just like that.'

He chuckled. Caspian returned the chuckle, raised a hand in farewell, and drove back into town.

Elaine Mancroft? The name and a number of questions occupied his mind until he reached Pall Mall, intending to lunch at his club. Elaine Mancroft — seeking some brief new sensation between the run of one play and the start of another? Acting out a part — or insinuating herself into the group in order to study some aspect of a subject which might be useful to her in a new role? Somewhere he had seen announcements of a forthcoming production. Perhaps it had already begun. He would verify it; perhaps risk an interview on some pretext connected with their mutual interest, the theatre.

As he pushed through the heavy swing doors of the Pantheon Club he was almost thrust backward by Joseph Hinde, snatching his hat from the porter and storming his way out.

'Caspian. Sorry.' They stood wedged between the weight of the two doors. 'Damn the man. Behind my back, seeing her, making everything ten times worse.'

A ponderous head surmounted the balcony rail of the first floor, high above. Caspian recognized the broad, exaggerated smile.

'Sir Andrew?' he ventured.

'Yes, Andrew, confound him. He's been to see Laura.'

'As her uncle, I suppose he wanted to see how she was progressing.'

'Progressing?' Hinde made no attempt to disguise his rage with any pontifical veneer. 'He has set her back quite appallingly. Comes to see her in my absence, and leaves her in a far worse state than before. He'll not set foot in my house again.'

He wrenched at one flap of the door and went furiously down the steps.

Sir Andrew Thornhill waited by the rail for Caspian to climb the stairs to the balcony. 'Extraordinary tantrums old Joseph throws when the mood takes him.'

'Miss Hinde is none too well. It must

be upsetting for him.'

'Been to see her myself,' said Thornhill heartily. 'Try to cheer her up. Needs it, heaven knows, in that gloomy place.'

'What did you say to her?' Caspian asked casually.

'She's always turned to me when she's been a bit down, you know. Misses her mother, and poor old Joseph doesn't do much to make up for it. Won't so much as talk about Florence when Laura needs it, and no attempt to share interests with her. I do what I can. There's a lot in that girl, you know. But no, I suppose you've never met her?'

'I've met her.'

'Then you know what I mean. But there I am trying to help her, and what thanks do I get from her own father?'

'I got the impression that your help effected little improvement in Miss Hinde's health.'

'There'll be no improvement until he lets her out of prison. That's what it is, old Nasmyth Lodge: a prison.'

'From which you hoped to let her out?'

'A ticket of leave, perhaps. That was all.

No wonder she's feeling down, refused even that. The way Joseph flies off . . . ' He laughed harshly, too eager for Caspian's collusion in a sneer against Hinde. 'You taking lunch here?'

There was the hint of an invitation. Caspian picked it up gladly. 'You'll join me? Or are you with friends?'

'Glad of your company.'

They went in together to a table in one of the windows overlooking the terrace behind the club, with a narrow glimpse of trees in St James's Park between two white walls. When the slices of raised game pie were on the table before them, Thornhill showed signs of changing the conversation and treating his audience to a lecture on one of his favourite topics — the inadequacy of the views of Hertz and his disciples on kinetic energy and light waves, and the misconceptions which he himself would set to rights if allowed to live long enough and complete his own experiments.

As he paused for breath, Caspian on impulse said: 'I have come here straight from the Camden Lecture Rooms.'

Thornhill, jabbing at a piece of pie with the fork, which a few seconds ago had been outlining theories in the air, was suddenly still. Then with a grunt he said: 'An odd time of day for lectures.'

'When your group ceased to meet there, where else did you go?'

'Group, my dear fellow?'

'I'm not sure whether you sent Miss Hinde the newspaper cutting anonymously, or passed it openly to her on the grounds of — how did you put it? — sharing interests. But I fancy you were there from the start. What's behind it?'

'I don't know what the deuce you're talking about, Caspian, but I certainly don't like your tone.'

'And what was the message you took to her that made her father so angry — and Miss Hinde so much the worse in herself?'

'This has gone too far.'

Thornhill made a move to get up. But there were several other tables between the window and the door, and all of them had filled up rapidly. Caspian had banked on this. He could not imagine Thornhill getting up and creating a disturbance in the middle of the meal, with all eyes upon him.

'Your niece is indeed ill. You're prepared to let her waste away rather than tell me what is wrong with her?'

'I'm a physicist, sir, not a physician. And as for your own presumption in — '

'She's willing herself to die. Or being willed to die. Are you silent because you daren't risk the same fate?'

'This is gibberish.'

'I agree. As a physicist, you would reject such nonsense out of hand. Am I not right?'

Thornhill, chewing like a small child unable to get rid of an uncomfortable mouthful, spluttered a harsher but less steady laugh than before. 'So Joseph's called you in to exorcize poor Laura's imagined demons? Joseph, of all men!'

Caspian tried to control his temper. He understood all too well how Joseph Hinde could be goaded into anger by this mixture of complacency and aggressiveness.

'Sir Andrew, you do know something

about Miss Hinde's activities since January. And when her father barred her from those activities, you did get a message to her, didn't you?'

'I'm not obliged to answer impertinent questions from someone outside the family.'

'You're a man of science, Sir Andrew.' Caspian reined himself in; tried another course, hating the need to flatter and cajole. 'A researcher of great distinction. I can't believe that you'd be easily bamboozled.'

'Hm.' Thornhill was clearly not going to be bamboozled now.

'However unorthodox the group you and Miss Hinde belong to, I find it hard to believe that a man of your calibre would surrender all his critical faculties to superstitions and threats. I beg you, Sir Andrew, if the girl allowed herself to be committed to something which you must know was damaging — '

'I've already told you I'll not discuss intimate family matters with any busybody from outside the family.' Thornhill clattered his knife and fork down. 'And if

I did belong to any serious private discussion group — if, I say — then I'd no more talk about it to a non-member than I'd betray a Masonic oath.'

'So it is a lodge of some kind.'

'Don't put words into my mouth.'

'A lodge which admits women,' said Caspian, 'or, even, is controlled by a woman?'

'You've no right to hector me, sir.'

'And you have no right,' said Caspian with muted ferocity, 'to condemn your own niece to death.'

'This is outrageous.'

'Either as a member of the family or as a man of science, you can't let yourself be bound by loyalty to some perverse hocus-pocus.'

'What are your precise qualifications, Dr. Caspian, for advising me on scientific matters?'

'I'm concerned for Mr. Hinde,' said Caspian, 'and for his daughter. And for your own sake I wouldn't wish to see you proven a murderer.'

'Outrageous,' said Thornhill.

'A murderer. For unless I know what

possesses her, I shall be unable to save her. And the responsibility will be yours as surely as if you had personally laid this illness upon her.'

Thornhill would endure no more. Rather than outface Caspian any longer, he chose to brave a few curious glances as, leaving his food half-finished, he pushed back his chair and strode across the dining room towards the door and the balcony.

Caspian's appetite, too, was gone. His stomach was racked by a colic of anger. It was still plaguing him when he reached home. He had handled that confrontation badly, and perhaps given away too much to a potentially dangerous enemy — to one who, whatever else he might claim, was at this stage an enemy of Laura's. But Thornhill's gross self-esteem had that effect on one.

How much did Thornhill admit to himself, what twisted ambitions and twisted procedures did he turn over in his mind, when he was alone?

When Bronwen returned late in the afternoon, Caspian was pacing up and down their small strip of garden. Explanation was swift and self-critical. Bronwen's intuition picked up the essential nuances and reservations without his having to put them too explicitly into words.

'I'm convinced that Thornhill is implicated,' he concluded. 'I can feel the whole temper of it. But he can't see that he's trapped, just as surely as Laura Hinde is trapped.'

Bronwen paused by the sundial. Abstractedly she picked shreds of moss from a letter in the motto encircling the dial: *For our time is a very shadow that passeth away.*

She said: 'I could see how those inbred folk who nearly brought about our death in the fens would bow to savage old traditions. But the sort of man we're dealing with here — '

'Is just as susceptible,' he took her up, 'provided you tempt him with the right phrases. Talk to such men in their own high-flown language, and they're as gullible as their most primitive predecessors. Describe Beelzebub in mathematical terms and they'll acknowledge him as a natural force. Don't talk of possession by evil spirits but of metabolic disturbances and the divided psyche, and the nineteenth-century Harley Street medical man will feel at home with your jargon. Each of us has his own vanity — the assurance that we're too modern and too well-educated to be hoodwinked into surrendering our critical faculties. The vanity itself is the worst danger. It's simply a matter of finding the most sensitive intellectual point and applying the right pressure. Your scientists are subject to the same crude fears and appetites as any lonely peasant. They'll gladly find whatever you choose they shall find; and find the most erudite justifications for what their ordinary impulses drive them to do.'

'What will Thornhill's justification be,' she wondered, 'for letting his niece die?'

'Perhaps that she wouldn't accept his advice, so has only herself to blame.'

'You think there'll be another attempt to reach her?'

'I don't know if there needs to be. Thornhill's visit may have been her last chance, and now they can safely leave her

to her own guilt. With that self-induced
Ilona firmly established in her, she'll soon
accomplish her own destruction.'

'And if Ilona's an outside figure and
not one of Laura's hallucinations at all?'

'Still determined to force that outsider
on us?' He tried to make a pleasantry of
it.

'She forced herself on us.'

Arguments assembled neatly on his
tongue but remained unuttered. He
thought back to the caretaker and that
talk of the lady who always wore a veil
and knew he was arguing against
something which grew hourly too strong
for disbelief.

★   ★   ★

The brougham edged through a crush of
vehicles before the Mansion House, and
at last found a gap through which to escape.
Rigorous believer in a strict timetable for
himself and everyone else, Joseph Hinde
growled his displeasure. Traffic was growing worse every week, but he could not
bear the grit and smell of suburban trains.

He was sorry for those who had to use such transport in and out of the tempestuous sprawl of London, and was the first to support parliamentary legislation to ease their lot; but he preferred not to experience it at first hand more often than could be helped.

The final trot through Fulham and Hammersmith was brisk and comfortable. Hinde took his gold half-hunter from his waistcoat and nodded. They would go through the gates of Nasmyth Lodge at the moment he had ordained.

Then, just as his coachman was about to make the slight turn out into the road preparatory to approaching the gates, they slowed and stopped. A gig and a carrier's wagon had collided on the corner, the gig tipping over towards the pavement, the carrier's horse pawing the ground awkwardly as if it had lost a shoe.

A woman stood by the lodge gates, watching. And past her, as Hinde let down his window and leaned out for a better appraisal of the accident, walked Laura.

Incredulous, he called out. The coachman leaned down.

'Won't take a minute, sir. I'll ease my way round — '

'Laura!'

The girl did not turn her head. But the woman by the gates stepped abruptly forward, her arms extended.

A baker's delivery van swung round the locked vehicles on the wrong side of the road, and mounted the pavement. The woman seemed to throw herself at its side, pushing with outstretched hands. Laura was suddenly falling towards the skidding wheel of the van, falling . . . and then was obscured by the canvas side of the vehicle as it squealed to a halt.

5

The temple reared bright and graceful from its knoll, and a streak of light along the surface of the river sparkled between two of its columns. Set back within the arc of the colonnade, the marble draperies of a goddess were half in shadow, half a virginal whiteness. Bronwen contrived to get the figure into the centre of her picture and at the same time to include the little cupola and, beyond it, a high palisade of poplars and one smudge of lowering cloud.

She moved the camera into a fresh position, this time taking in the west wing of the house itself.

'Are we in your way?'

Two heads turned. Laura Hinde got up from a chair in the shelter of the terrace and shaded her eyes. Beside her, Mrs. Relph prodded a cushion in her Bath chair and settled into a more comfortable position.

'Please don't move,' Bronwen called back. 'You make a very pretty touch — figures in a landscape.'

Mrs. Relph folded her hands in her lap and smiled.

When she had finished, Bronwen walked across the lawn to join them.

Now was the time she should have been taking those portraits of Laura. The girl's face and whole manner had been transformed. Within a matter of days the colour had returned to her cheeks, her eyes were alive and responsive. Every other minute she would turn to her companion and say something, listen, interrupt gleefully and laugh — not so much at their conversation as from sheer spontaneous pleasure.

'Mrs. Relph has made an incredible difference,' Hinde had said. 'I simply cannot credit it.'

Nor could Caspian, when he heard. Which was why his wife was here at Nasmyth Lodge, though she made a great show of being concerned solely with her camera and the composition of scenes inside and outside the house.

Now she said: 'If you'd move further into the sun, before we lose it behind that cloud, I could make a charming little study.'

'With me as an old lady on her way to take the waters? I'm not sure I'd find it flattering.'

Temporarily confined to the wheelchair, Mrs. Relph could in no circumstances have posed as an old lady. In her late twenties, she certainly looked more mature than Laura, with shadows of experience in the corners of her mouth and slightly wistful wrinkles under her eyes — but these might, after all, be no more than the legacy of an intense foreign sun. Her mouth was full and generous; her eyes, deep blue when she turned her head one way, changed almost to violet when they caught the light from another direction. Her complexion, though darkened and mildly freckled here and there by the years abroad, was smooth and in some indefinable way hazed over as if she were ever so faintly out of focus. Yet her voice was clear and precise, and her grip when she first shook hands with Bronwen had been firm.

'A souvenir,' said Laura fondly, 'of heroic

deeds. Yes, I'd love to have a picture of you as the wounded heroine.'

'For when I've gone?'

The girl's face darkened, but then she was laughing and insistent again. 'Who's talking of your going?'

'I can't stay here forever.'

'It's a nice enough place to stay. Now that you're here, it's the nicest possible place.'

'As soon as my knee improves — only a few days, your doctor says — I must cease to be a burden.'

'I shall die.' Laura said it jokingly, with no apparent awareness that she could ever have uttered such words in the past and meant them.

Bronwen looked down the drive towards the gates with the air of one considering a landscape study. Then, as if the thought had just idly occurred to her, she said: 'What were you going out for, that day?'

'I don't know.' Laura shrugged. 'Funny, isn't it — I really don't remember a thing about it.'

Bronwen sensed that it was true. All memory of the impulse that had urged the girl out of her stupor and driven her to evade the nurse and hurry through the gates had fled.

'The shock probably drove it all out of your head,' observed Mrs. Relph.

And many other things besides, Bronwen marvelled.

'If you had come past two minutes earlier,' Laura was saying, 'or two minutes later — '

'Then I'd not be here now, making a nuisance of myself.'

'And I might not even be here at all. And apart from that, suppose we'd never met? Because without that, we wouldn't have done.'

Mrs. Relph gave Bronwen a gently conspiratorial smile. Let Laura chatter on. She had been ill, she was well, let her pour it all out. There was no harm in this impetuous outburst of girlish sentimentality. No possible harm.

Reminiscently Mrs. Relph said: 'My father once told me that if he'd not missed a particular boat to Bombay, he wouldn't have had a little difference of opinion with the Company, and so would not have been posted to a different province. And, more important, he would never have met my mother.'

Bronwen nodded. 'Because it rains one day when we expected it to be fine, we stay indoors and miss a garden party where one chance acquaintanceship might have altered the rest of our life. Or a man lets a chemical retort boil over and thereby makes a discovery which might otherwise have had to wait a hundred years.'

'Fate!' cried Laura.

'Or chance.'

'Aren't they the same?' said Mrs. Relph. The wickerwork of her chair creaked as she turned to look full at Laura, affectionate yet speculative. 'In India the sages teach that there are no chance encounters or chance decisions along the path to fulfilment. One comes to a crossroads intending to go straight on, and then something makes one turn left. But in fact that has been ordained from the beginning. Our footsteps are guided: to cross a road and meet somebody unexpectedly . . . or not to cross the road, and so never meet them at all . . . '

To stand by lodge gates, thought Bronwen, when a girl comes blindly through them, and to rescue her from an impending accident . . .

Chance.

'I don't believe it,' Caspian had said flatly.

It was too neat that such a bystander should have been there when Laura was running away from home; that she should have appeared to throw herself at Laura, and then be shown to have saved Laura; and that she should have pulled a ligament in one of her knees and be invited to stay in the house for a few days until it was safe to put her weight to the ground again. Of course if it had not been Mrs. Relph it might have been someone else. Or it might have been nobody, and then Laura might have been killed. Chance? 'It's too convenient,' Caspian fretted. 'Another messenger, d'you suppose?' It was time, he decreed, that Bronwen should take up Hinde's polite invitation to visit his home and add studies of the house and grounds to the collection of architectural photographs started by her father. With the run of the premises for a day, she must see what she could make of this newcomer.

What Bronwen made of her was warm and uncomplicated. Laura's gushing affection was balanced by the other woman's quiet tolerance — and by a steadier yet just as instinctive affection. Somehow Mrs. Relph's presence had cancelled out Laura's self-torturing past and put everything in a new perspective.

If chance, then a happy one.

Mr. Hinde came out on the terrace and down the stone steps. He stood by a stone urn, some feet away, as if not presuming to intrude on the group of younger folk; yet he, too, looked at ease and part of this new contentment. It was all too quick and too perfect; but Bronwen could have no doubt of the genuineness of Mrs. Relph and the effect she had on her companions.

Mrs. Relph was looking dreamily across the gardens to where a rowing boat was crossing the river at a tangent. Mr. Hinde's gaze lingered on her profile.

Then shadow flowed across the lawn,

splashing against the terrace and over their heads and shoulders. Mrs. Relph shivered and drew a silk shawl closer about her throat.

At once Mr. Hinde said: 'I think we'd better wheel you indoors, dear lady.'

'I'm afraid I've still not readjusted to the climate. This has been my first English winter for five years.'

Hinde was about to take charge of the Bath chair, but Laura hurried forward. Her hand touched Mrs. Relph's arm and for a moment rested there. Bronwen sensed the contact like an electric spark bridging a gap. Then Laura was turning the chair dexterously towards the door at the end of the wing.

Her father watched them go. 'A plucky young woman.'

'You must feel very indebted to her.'

'The whole country is in the debt of such ladies. Husband killed in his country's service, you know.'

'I gathered she was a widow, but I'd no idea — '

'Killed in action, like my own boy. Not a soldier, you understand: a good ICS family, the Relphs. Poor lad. Died in what sounds like some damnably unnecessary dispute while on tour as an Assistant Collector. Still too painful for her to say much, of course.'

His doting enthusiasm was as fresh and unforeseen as Laura's release from her trance.

'And doing Laura a world of good.' Mr. Hinde wanted nothing more than to talk on about his guest. 'A world of good. Takes her out of herself. What she's always needed.'

Gathering clouds and a hint of rain made further photography impossible. When Bronwen was ready to leave, two footmen were sent to carry her impedimenta to the carriage. At the last moment Mr. Hinde took her to one side.

'Do come again whenever it pleases you, Mrs. Caspian. I mean it: do come. As you'll have observed, the atmosphere here has improved remarkably. Perhaps you'd tell your husband just how much it has improved. And shall we tell him my daughter's illness appears to have run its course? I doubt there's any purpose in his pursuing his line of treatment.'

As she was driven away, father and daughter waved from the portico, their free arms linking together.

'It's all too sudden,' said Caspian when she had finished her account. 'Ready-made bliss at such short notice? No hint of a false note anywhere?'

'At one moment I fancied there was something, but I was just being over-suspicious.'

'Ilona?' The name went off like a squib between them.

She shook her head. 'I'm sure I'd have heard.'

'All along you've been the one insisting on a mysterious woman outside Laura. Now a mightily mysterious one walks right into the household, and you get not the faintest hint that the whole thing's been contrived and Laura's being seduced anew?'

'No.' Bronwen spoke with growing conviction. 'I did listen for those false notes. But I really believe it was a genuine accident — '

'Turned to good purpose by the

woman who had in any case been waiting there for Laura, knowing for some reason that she would come.'

'A genuine intervention by a casual bystander,' Bronwen insisted, 'and a genuine stroke of luck for Laura Hinde and her father.'

Briefly they let their minds intermingle, and she let him draw from her the assurance of Laura's happiness and new-found security.

'It's all very well.' He slumped back in his chair. 'If it's really true, will the cure be a lasting one? What will happen to Laura when this Mrs. Relph is well enough to leave?'

★ ★ ★

The insidious voice trickled out of the water jug along with the water pouring into the brandy glass.

'Come and talk to me, Elaine.'

'No.' She put the jug down, drank, and stood quite still so that the voice would have no sound with which to confuse itself. It wasn't really there; and if she made no sound, there would be nothing for it to distort.

A cart rattled slowly along the street below. She hurried to close the window tightly, but already the noise had struck its own rhythm.

'I'm waiting to hear from you, Elaine. Waiting to see you, Elaine.'

'You can wait forever.'

'You'll have to come sooner or later.'

Never. I'll never come. Not into earth and slime and the rotting embrace of Adelaide.

Elaine Mancroft turned to her dressing table and stared in anguish at her face in the mirror; then turned quickly away, fearful lest another face might look over her shoulder. So far there had been no direct confrontation with Adelaide. If she clearly saw as well as hearing Adelaide, that would surely drive her mad.

There was half-an-hour left before she was due to leave for the theatre. If she hurried to get ready now and asked for the carriage to be sent round early, she could leave this infested house behind. But then there would be the tension of waiting in the theatre, arriving too soon in that atmosphere which would thicken around her, so that by the time she had to go on stage she would be suffocating and the words would have escaped her again. She had survived this last triumphant week: she could continue only if she timed her arrival to a split second and made her first entrance without a backward look.

Daniel ought to be beside her. But he asserted that, since his presence seemed to make her nervous, she was best left alone; he had an actor to interview, a touring manager to see. Or was there a girl somewhere, training to step into Elaine Mancroft's shoes?

The voice came again. She stiffened against it; then knew it was not the same voice.

It had never been her intention to go to the theatre this evening. A prior appointment — how could she have forgotten?

Elaine laughed. She finished her brandy, not desperately but jubilantly. The ordeal that lay ahead was the culmination of all those weeks of listening and longing. She had waited, and learned, and now it was her turn. After tonight there would be no echoes of Adelaide. Adelaide would have to wait for eternity. Tonight's ordeal was nothing to be feared.

She had been promised.

It was a good omen that, for the first time in history, Mrs. Wraxall did not hear her come downstairs and go down the garden to the mews gate. Briggs was not in the stable harnessing the carriage horses yet. She led the mare to the curricle and backed it between the shafts, and was away across the cobbles before anyone could wonder what possessed her.

Going to a cemetery, to banish death: what would Daniel make of such a theme? Perhaps one day she would offer it to him, when she was sure that he had been completely recaptured.

She had not been along this route since Adelaide's funeral, but she knew every inch of the way. The curricle rolled steadily on, unfaltering. She felt all the confidence and anticipation she had felt when driving from a small railway station deep in Sussex for her first secret rendezvous with Daniel. Later their meetings had grown more blatant and defiant; and Adelaide more drunken. She wondered how she would feel on the return drive through these same streets: whether she would be conscious of a physical change, or some ecstatic liberation of the spirit.

There was a lane beside the graveyard, with tethering posts under the trees at the end. She remembered, with a clarity that surprised her, a side gate for mourners leaving their vehicles at that spot. It ought surely to be locked at night; but she was less surprised to find it open. Of course everything would have been arranged.

She went in.

There was no moon, but the light of the sky itself and a reflected glow from the gas, naphtha and incandescent electric lamps of London picked out arrays of stone blocks forming an interminable ancient monument, marching away in ranks to the night horizon, broken here and there by majestic figures rising like heavenly sentinels. Elaine made out a path, and followed it between soot-encrusted headstones. Here and there a recent addition gleamed bare and cold.

Adelaide had been buried in a corner sheltered by a yew hedge and one stooping tree. Here there was permanent shadow. Elaine stopped at an intersection of paths, peering into the gloom. She could just make out the stone and the white surround of the grave. Through the central darkness she seemed almost able to see the coffin beneath the surface, and a glint of the brass handles. She blinked. There was another faint gleam of metal: a spade had been propped against the tree.

Her knees were trembling but she forced herself to walk into the shadows.

There was a darker shape, which had not been here before, the shape of a dark angel standing beside the stone — an angel with her countenance veiled.

It was just as it had been when she waited in the wings, unable to take another step. She had forgotten her lines. She dared not go any further.

'Do you wish to turn back?' The voice was as unyielding as the granite and marble headstones.

She tried to answer her cue. 'No.'

'You must endure the earth before the rebirth.'

'I will endure.'

'Of your own free will.'

She stared at that dark rectangle and saw that the surface had been disturbed and turned over, so that a shallow trough lay down the centre of the plot. She licked her dry lips. 'Of my own free will.'

'Gladly.'

She thought of the curtain coming down on this tragic act, and rising again upon a triumphant future. In a voice that all London would have known to be Elaine Mancroft's she said: 'Gladly.'

'Then come.'

Elaine walked those last few yards and stared into the pit.

It would soon be over. She would begin the ordeal freely and courageously, and go through fear to joy; and if there was no applause but her own to greet her as she rose from the earth, that would be sufficient for once.

She felt herself falling. Darkness rose to meet her. She closed her eyes, jarring to one side as her shoulder struck the edge of the open grave. Then she was face down in the earth. It was damper than it ought to have been: damp as though it had been saturated just before she came. When she opened her mouth to cry out, slime oozed into it. She groped out desperately, and felt stinging agony in one finger. Her nail must have caught in the more solid sides of the grave and been twisted. She tried to make herself lie still, to accept, to await release. Let the earth embrace her symbolically: that was what all this meant — a symbolic surrender before the promised freedom. That was all.

She felt an odd tug at her hair.

* * *

'No,' said Count Caspar, 'I have no intention of selling the theatre. You've no cause for alarm. But neither do I intend to undertake major productions in person.'

Louis Mordecai sighed. 'We've built one or two very clever little items, Doctor. Very cunning.'

'I'm sure you have. And with a team of performers such as you've got at the moment, I'm sure they'll be brilliantly used.'

'People still ask when you're going to do another season of your own.'

'They'll have to go on asking.'

Mordecai, senior craftsman and mainstay of the Cavern of Mystery, tried to look reproachful. His face was unfortunately not adapted for such expressions: sallow and shrivelled, it was essentially the face of a monkeyish little gnome perpetually devising new mischief, magic and deceptions in his own corner of the cave.

Caspian tried not to reveal how sorely he was tempted. Setting foot in the workshops of the theatre which he had so painstakingly built up, smelling the wood and the paint and the whole indefinable breath of the place, he could so easily slip back into the personality of Count Caspar — Master of Prestidigitation and Illusion, as he had been billed.

The itch to perform again, to provoke the gasps and shuddering silences, and the then the irresistible applause of the audience, was a torment.

He resisted. That flamboyant phase of his career had ended, of his own choice, when he married Bronwen. Together they had lived through some days of terror that made all else seem trivial. Stage illusions had become too easy: he had grown too skilful, and those skills were needed elsewhere.

'You haven't seen this one, now?' Mordecai lured him to one end of the workshop.

Fastened to the wall was a huge wheel with twelve segments in different colours, each marked with a sign of the zodiac. Mordecai touched the rim with one finger and began to spin it smoothly. The signs and colours blurred and then separated again, slowing.

'We'll have a man down in the audience asking questions but not conveying them directly to the magician on stage. The old mentalist routine, of course.'

'Of course,' said Caspian.

The wheel slowed to a stop, with a long metal arrow pointing from above at the sign of Aquarius.

'Your birth sign I think?' Mordecai's

sharp chin jabbed upwards in challenge.

'As you very well know.'

'You didn't see me touch the wheel after it started spinning? Didn't see me go anywhere near it?'

'If I had, I'd have reprimanded you for getting slack in my absence.'

Mordecai giggled. 'There's a brake, of course, and a segment lock. The magician and his confederate in the auditorium use the mentalist alphabet and 'Hurry up' codes, naturally. We're working out a shortened version to communicate dates, but while the wheel's rotating we'll have time to throw in any prompts that may be needed, and stop the wheel only when the full message is received. Or we might just possibly try the pasteboard and stencil method — see which works best. And we'll answer one personal question each, and cast a good-luck horoscope. It'll be called the Wheel of Fortune.'

'Very original,' said Caspian dryly. He tugged at his jutting beard. 'I've always dissociated myself from any spiritualism and fortune-telling. I'm not sure I favour this.'

'But they'll know this is professional trickery. And that'll make them more suspicious about any fortune-teller who claims not to be a trickster.'

'Hm.' Caspian remained dubious; but he could hardly criticize while at the same time declaring his own non-participation in future programmes. As they turned away from the wheel, he said: 'How do you trigger the brake and lock? Someone behind the scenes?'

'There wasn't anybody behind there a minute ago, when we gave you your Aquarius, was there?'

'Obviously not. A foot control of some kind, then?'

Slyly Mordecai suggested: 'Would you like to examine the mechanism in detail, Doctor? You'd maybe have some refinements to contribute.'

'No.' Caspian skirted the trap. 'I've come here merely to collect a few bits and pieces from the storeroom. Nothing too big, don't worry — small conjuring tricks, nothing that'll wreck your stage show.'

'I'll come and open the room for you.'

Mordecai watched without a word as

143

Caspian chose two packs of cards, the impedimenta for the coin multiplication routine, some slates and tracing paper and a bottle of ink. Locking up again, his curiosity got the better of him: 'Going to do some home entertaining?'

Caspian shook his head.

'A Saturday night house dinner at the Savage Club, perhaps?'

Caspian tantalized him with silence.

Mordecai plodded beside his employer to the stage door; and there Caspian put him out of his misery.

'I'm giving a lecture at Scotland Yard to a group of detectives specializing in race-course and gaming frauds. They promise to supply their own roulette wheel, so I need not encumber myself with that.'

Leicester Square was bright and busy in the morning sunshine. Caspian waved a cab from the rank on the comer, and the driver wove an experienced way round the worst of the traffic and along Panton Street, past the Comedy Theatre.

'Stop!'

The cabby reined in. 'Here? You left something behind?'

'I'm sorry. Put me down.' Caspian swung his case to the pavement and took out a handful of small change. 'I don't think I should ask you to wait.'

The cabby glanced at the money and touched his snuff-brown bowler. 'Right you are, sir. You know best.'

Two notice boards which had attracted Caspian's attention were propped against the front of the theatre, declaring in large hand-lettered capitals:

NO PERFORMANCE THIS EVENING
OWING TO ILLNESS
REOPENING SHORTLY

To either side, even more prominent, were playbills carrying the name of Elaine Mancroft.

He walked down the alley to the stage door.

A harassed-looking man with a mauve-spotted bald head was stumping from the direction of the stage to the little office by the door, muttering under his breath. He glared at the newcomer, then gave a grudging little flip of the fingers to a non-existent cap on his head.

'And what can I do for you, sir?'

'I've just seen the boards outside. There's nothing wrong with Miss Mancroft, is there?'

'Nobody's said so, not that I know of,' said the doorkeeper cautiously.

'But to postpone a performance . . . '

'What is it, Jenks?' A man in a close-buttoned reefer jacket and check trousers came from the end of the passage. He came up and moved round Caspian to see him in a better light. Caspian recognized him as Daniel Clegg, playwright and manager; and in the same instant was himself recognized. 'Hah! Count Caspar, isn't it?'

'That is so.'

'We don't need a juggler in this establishment, thank you.'

'I was hoping to see Miss Mancroft.'

'She's indisposed.'

'Nothing serious, I trust?'

'What concern is it of yours?'

'It's rather urgent that I see her. Is she at home?'

Clegg's mouth twitched. He had difficulty in controlling it. 'If you'll tell me what it is you want to discuss, I'm sure I can — '

'She has disappeared,' said Caspian. 'Fled from home. She may be in some danger!'

'Is this some vulgar trick to draw attention to your Cavern of Mystery?'

Caspian said bluntly: 'How much do you know about the occult society she joined earlier this year?'

'It's not for me to keep note of all Miss Mancroft's interests outside the theatre.' But Clegg was troubled. 'Something occult, you say?'

'Something that may be taking her over.'

'Taking her over? Yes, that's the impression . . . her bad dreams, and getting her lines wrong, and those insane accusations . . . ' He looked wary; then drew Caspian further down the corridor away from the doorman. 'Yes, I wouldn't put it past her. What sort of thing did this society practise?'

'I'm trying to find out.'

'You mean it's no more than some theory of yours?'

'So far I know of one young woman who came close to death. She, too, tried to run from home. But she was held back, and we hope her danger is over.'

'What put you on to Elaine?'

Caspian evaded this. 'You talked of her bad dreams, and insane accusations. What did she say?'

'She's been mumbling for weeks about death and corruption . . . and she's so scared of dying.'

'So are most of us.'

'But we don't dwell on it every minute of the day. Dying, and being buried, and still being alive. She keeps telling me she wants to be immortal because she daren't die. I've tried joking with her, telling her she'll be immortal — through my plays. But she goes on about not being able to face what may be waiting for her.'

'What — or who?'

'Oh, I see what you're driving at,' said Clegg shakily. 'My wife, and her death, and . . . oh, all the gossip, the tittle-tattle. You've heard all about it.'

'In our profession, Mr. Clegg, one does hear things in dramatic, if not always accurate, detail. So you think Miss Mancroft has been haunted by some sense of guilt which she couldn't shake off?'

'There was nothing to feel guilty about. Neither of us has any reason for guilt.'

'But she may have thought she had.'

Clegg stared at something or someone beyond Caspian. He said: 'Adelaide's grave. You don't suppose . . . she couldn't . . . ?'

They went out together, and Clegg made no protest when Caspian climbed into the hansom with him. The drive seemed interminable. Twice Clegg started to say something, then gagged on it. At last he managed: 'If she did have these strange persuasions, and mixed with those other cranks, what would she be expected to do?'

'It's more a matter of what she would want to do. There may have been certain rituals in which she was persuaded to take part in order to exorcize her fears.'

They reached the cemetery. Clegg croaked instructions for being driven round to the side gate. As they walked through it and approached his late wife's grave they saw that somebody else was already there. A man with a spade was leaning incredulously over the grave.

Clegg strode up to him. 'What d'you think you're playing at?'

Lying face down in a shallow trough was Elaine Mancroft, one arm outstretched. Her head was twisted to one side to show her left eye, smeared with earth and a handful of grass.

'Nothing to do with me, sir. Only just come across it a minute ago, and that's the truth.'

Caspian stooped over the corpse. The hair was tangled in the dirt, but there was one spot on the scalp where a tuft appeared to have been torn away. A nail was missing from one bloodied finger of the outstretched hand: most likely, he surmised, torn out when she groped for support.

But why should she have plunged into that makeshift grave in the first place — and why found it impossible to scramble upright again?

Clegg was raging: 'Who dug that surface up? That spade — '

'The spade's one of mine, sir. But I didn't use it for this, I swear I didn't. We don't disturb the dead, sir, not here we don't. More'n our jobs are worth. I noticed it missing from the shed and went looking for it, and there it was leaning against that tree when I crossed the path. But it wasn't till I got right up to it that I knew anything about . . . about that.'

Clegg was swaying perilously above Elaine Mancroft's body. 'She came up here? Up here?' he repeated in wonderment. 'Came up here and dug a hole for herself — and threw herself on top of Adelaide and just let herself die?' He stared at Caspian across the disordered grave. 'You said something about her being persuaded. By whom?'

'That's what I'm anxious to find out,' said Caspian, 'before the influence is concentrated upon somebody else.'

★　★　★

The verdict was one of death by misadventure. If most people, including the coroner, considered that Elaine Mancroft had made a sketchy attempt to dig her own grave so that she might then commit suicide, there was no conclusive evidence on this latter point; and it was regarded as a worthy gesture to the memory of a much-adored actress that such a disagreeable matter should not be pursued. Obituaries were fulsome and extensive, and the funeral announcements inserted by Daniel Clegg in the leading newspapers were prose poems in their own right. It was not, however, the literary style which caught Caspian's attention. Turning from one paragraph to another, he said: 'She was born on a 23rd of April and died on the 23rd of April.'

'An unhappy coincidence,' said Bronwen.

'In this sort of thing there may be no more coincidences than, according to your Mrs. Relph, there are chance encounters or chance decisions.'

'She's hardly my Mrs. Relph. And I fail to see what — '

'Laura Hinde's birthday was on the 24th of March. That we know because of those birthday photographs. When do you suppose Sir Andrew Thornhill was born?'

Bronwen got up from her chair and went to the shelf of reference books. 'He's sure to be in Who's Who.'

'Tell me,' commanded Caspian softly,

'that it comes between the 21st of May and the 21st of June.'

She turned a page. Her gaze ran down the column, then rose to meet his. She said: 'The 25th of May.'

Not for the first time in recent weeks Caspian said: 'I don't believe it.' The words did not ring true. The zodiac wheel from the Cavern of Mystery workshop spun in his mind, and slowed, and he said: 'But I could be tempted to believe that *somebody* believes it.'

6

The number of members in the House to hear the Right Honourable Joseph Hinde's speech on obscene publications and declining moral standards was only just enough to constitute a quorum. One or two, having drunk too freely before stumbling to their seats, were asleep and fitfully snoring.

Thundering to the end of his peroration, Hinde flourished a folded copy of a magazine.

'This sort of filth, this provocation of lust: is it to be bought abroad and smuggled shamefacedly into this once unsullied country of ours? Is it an expensive periodical of limited circulation, for sale only to a circle of well-to-do rakes? No, it is not. It is freely available in towns and cities throughout the land. The corruption spreads. Every foul alley in the Metropolis reeks with it, and even the remotest hamlet.' He brandished the copy of *The Boudoir* at his audience. 'What are we to make of publications as lewd as this?'

'Pass it round,' said a wakeful wag on the Opposition benches, 'and perhaps we can advise.'

'At the end of a career in the service of our Queen and country, how many of us will be able to feel, if this day we make specious excuses for turning down the measures which I propose, that among the millions of our fellow citizens we can claim to have left a little more moral dignity than when we set our hand to the task? And if we cannot truthfully say that, then what right have we to speak here, make decisions here, and vote here?'

The debate that followed was partly flippant, partly sententious. Two sleeping members awoke, looked startled at finding themselves where they were, and left the chamber. One backbencher of Hinde's own party delivered a cynical little warning to all who presumed to dictate or limit the pleasures of others. The mood of the House was not entirely against the idea of forming a special committee: perhaps some members hoped, if chosen to serve on it, to be given the opportunity of inspecting books and folios of drawings which might otherwise have eluded them; but there was little overt enthusiasm for the motion.

A member of the Opposition was on his feet. 'Mr. Speaker, it is my duty to draw your attention to the fact that there are now insufficient Honourable Members present to form a quorum.'

The Speaker rose. 'Strangers will withdraw.' The division bells rang; he waited for the ordained four minutes for a few reluctant figures to return to the chamber, and counted. 'Thirty-seven.'

The sitting was adjourned.

Furious, Hinde went out in search of his carriage. Now he would be compelled to start all over again. There were times when he felt that all Parliamentary procedure was a mockery, designed to frustrate all possibility of reform. He had been slighted; but they had not heard the last of him.

He was still clutching the magazine. It was not the sort of thing he would have cared to leave about for the benefit of prurient, prying eyes. When, automatically, he straightened out its creases, it fell open at an illustrated page.

What was so appalling was that so many of the coloured lithographs were so competently done. Crudity often destroyed lust. But this well-drawn and well-printed stuff was shameful in the sheer craftsmanship of its creators.

The girl stood in a pose that could almost have been that of the virginal goddess in the colonnade of his own classical temple at Nasmyth Lodge. But there were no concealing draperies. Her proportions were similar to those of Elizabeth Relph.

Hinde slapped the pages shut. It was a monstrous thought. It was an insult to her even to think of her in such terms.

He closed his eyes. That made things worse.

As the brougham swept through his gates he looked out to seek relief from the purity of the temple goddess. But shadows of the pillars, flickering on the white marble body as the coach followed the curve of the drive, brought the stone to life. The bleached arms were moving, blood would flow through them, the scalloped skirt would drop.

It was appalling. Were all his Parliamentary speeches hypocrisy? In fighting to suppress other people's vices, was he really seeking only to deny his own?

The horse clopped to a standstill. He descended, fighting down his unruly impulses just as his wife had always, with a tremor of disgust, shamed him into fighting them down.

When the door opened he half expected to see her there now, welcoming him home: an invariably cool, civilized welcome; a polite enquiry about the progress of government or business in the City.

In the doorway stood Elizabeth Relph.

She was wearing a velveteen pelisse, with a ruching of dark maroon ribbon, and a gable bonnet. One gloved hand rested on the silver-topped cane, which he had offered her when she began to walk again.

Laura's gig came round the corner of the building from the stables, with Laura driving.

It was then that he saw the two small cases and the hatbox just within the hall.

'You're not leaving?'

'I have waited for you to return,' said

Mrs. Relph, 'so that I might make my farewells.'

'But to go so soon, the moment I set foot in the house!'

'I thought it best.'

Her eyes were sad but sure, beneath the jaunty peak of her bonnet. He was the first to lower his gaze. She had not been unaware of his feelings, then: aware of them, perhaps, before he himself acknowledged them, and been repelled by them. Her husband dead within this past twelvemonth, and she being dismayed by the glances and clumsy attentions of another . . .

Hinde wanted to seize her and insist she must stay. His home, his garden, his dinner table — what could they be without her? As she stood there, waiting for Sedgwick to have her cases brought out, he saw, like an aura shining with every second of her sojourn here, the memory of her sitting in the Bath chair, smiling, coaxing Laura back to life; talking to him quietly and movingly, over a glass of wine, about her life in India and her husband's death — a death on the sweltering plains near Sardarshalir, in some tragically unnecessary scuffle, while she passed the worst weeks up in the cooler hills at Chakrata; waiting up for him that time, two or three evenings ago, when the House had been forced to sit late.

Now she stood in his portico preparing to leave.

'Your maid?' He was at a loss for anything else to say.

'She went on ahead to prepare my rooms. I must not trespass any longer on your hospitality. And it's time I looked to my future — time to make a few decisions. Not impulsive ones!' A boy carried her cases out, proudly balancing the hatbox on one of them with his elbow. She said: 'I hope you won't mind Laura's driving me home. And I hope you'll let her come to visit. I should not wish to be deprived of her now.'

Or I of you, he said. But did not dare say it aloud.

He heard himself declare: 'My carriage is here. If you're determined to leave us, I'll accompany you myself.'

'I've arranged everything, Father,' said Laura quietly.

'Things can be rearranged.'

'Mr. Hinde,' said Mrs. Relph, 'I'd like to familiarize Laura with the route, so that she will have no difficulty in finding me again.'

The two women were making the decisions, and he was left standing beside the gig. When she was settled in it, Elizabeth Relph took off her glove and let her fingers rest in his for a moment. She had a strange, distraught look — as if, like himself, she found it impossible to believe that these recent days should be ending so conventionally.

She said: 'Don't worry about Laura. I'll see she comes safely home.'

★ ★ ★

Caspian dealt out the three cards slowly and deliberately on the table. The two volunteers facing him had not allowed themselves a single blink as he set the cards down.

'Well?' he challenged.

The others in the room edged closer.

The policeman on the left moistened his lips and then pointed.

'She's there.'

Caspian turned the card face uppermost. It was the nine of diamonds.

'And again?'

His hands skimmed above the cards, flicked one under another, turned the nine of diamonds face down again. Slowly and deliberately he separated them and nodded to the man on the right.

'Yes?'

The police officer grinned. He was quite confident. He had missed nothing this time. His right forefinger tapped the back of the middle card.

Again it was the nine of diamonds.

'Let me show you,' said Caspian.

Three times over he demonstrated the art of concealing the queen, and made each pupil go through it. Then he invited a bet on the joker in a full pack, sprayed it out on the table, ran the gamut of his simplest tricks — tricks that cost the unwary traveller and over-confident gambler a fortune every year.

'The trouble is,' said Superintendent Priestley, 'that we haven't the men to watch every Brighton train going out and tip off the guard, or to cover every corner of every racecourse in the land.'

'And about racecourses, sir,' intervened a very respectful detective officer, 'do you think you could go through that touts' semaphore just once again?'

Once again he went through his repertoire of touts' and thieves' signalling devices, and then again: first slowly, then at high speed.

When he encouraged the officers to try the brisk gestures for themselves, their hands collided in mid-air, there were a couple of winces of protest, and then a burst of applause.

'We're most grateful to you, Doctor,' said Superintendent Priestley as Caspian collected up his demonstration material. 'Every day some rogue contrives some new dodge to bedevil us. Short of taking you on the strength as our full-time fraud detector, I don't see how we can do without these regular lessons from you. The men appreciate it, make no mistake.'

'They make a very acute audience. I have to perform at least twice as well as usual in order to deceive them.'

'Well, sir, I've only one favour to ask.'

'And that is . . . ?'

'Please don't join the other side. I'd hate you to be let loose on the public.'

They laughed. Then Caspian said: 'And now, I've a favour to ask of you.'

'Anything we can do, at any time.'

'I want to trace a man who would have been drowned, if he *has* been drowned yet, between the 9th of February and the 20th of March.'

Priestley stared. 'Either there's been a drowning or there hasn't.'

'That's part of the problem. I don't know if I've got things in the right order. One way, it's too late to save him — or possibly her. The other way there may be a chance.'

'Doctor, if there's any question of foul play — '

'Foul it may well be. But I doubt that it comes within the scope of the law: not your kind of law, that is.'

'You're talking in riddles.'

'Because I don't know the solution. It's possible that you can help me find it.'

'You'll have to give us more to go on.'

'A man or a woman,' said Caspian, 'may have drowned in a pond or a canal or even the Thames — though that could add any number of complications — between those two dates I gave. If an identifiable body has been found, and it can be established that the victim's birthday also fell between those dates, there's a fair chance it's what I'm looking for.'

The Superintendent frowned.

'You surmise all this about someone who may or may not have died. Yet you don't know if it's a man or a woman?'

'I need anything you can add.'

'We can go through the records of folk we've fished out from one place and another. This one will be in our area?'

'I'm pretty sure of that, yes.'

'You give the impression of it being something outside the law — outside our jurisdiction, or . . . ?'

Caspian said: 'I promise that if I find any criminal prosecution is justified, I'll let you know.'

'Very well. I'll do what I can. But if there was a body, and it went into the river and then went out with the tide — '

'Then we shall have lost one element,' said Caspian, 'and I shall be left guessing about the other three.'

'You leave me guessing too,' grumbled Priestley, 'and right out of my element.'

Caspian set off towards Cheyne Walk.

He might have started the policeman on a false trail. The death by drowning might still be in the future. But one had to start somewhere, try to establish a pattern, even if it had to be taken to pieces and reassembled later.

Caspian flexed his aching fingers. He was out of practice. Better, he thought, to devote himself to exercising his fingers and muscles and practical skills rather than exercising his mind on a task from which he had been courteously but categorically dismissed.

'Laura has shaken off all that nonsense of hers,' Hinde had said. 'I can see that she's completely recovered.' When Caspian asked about others who might be involved and still in danger, Hinde had made it clear that he regretted having paid even the vaguest lip service to such semi-mystical notions. The whole thing had been an aberration. Laura was his only concern; and Laura was cured, thanks to the friendship of Mrs. Relph. 'I may be unversed in occult matters, Dr. Caspian, but,' Hinde reiterated, 'I can see with my own eyes that Laura has recovered. She is well and safe.'

He would not have understood the compulsion that nagged Caspian to pursue the matter further. Hinde felt no concern for the lasting virulence of whatever it was that had fed on Laura and, like some plague carrier, might even now be settling on another.

Had that Ilona shadow sought and found another prey; or was it conceivably still hiding away in Laura, awaiting the moment to awaken and resume its cankerous feast?

Caspian let himself into the house as midnight was striking. He could feel the presence of Bronwen, waiting up for him.

And could feel her distress.

His pace quickened across the hall. She had been instantly aware of his arrival and was opening the sitting room door as he reached it.

She kissed him. In the room beyond stood Joseph Hinde. Caspian felt no immediate surprise. His thoughts had been on the man, and now thought carried over unbroken into the sight of him.

'I may have made a terrible mistake,' he was saying. 'A fatal misjudgment.'

'Mr. Hinde has been waiting for you,' said Bronwen. 'I've been trying to tell him she's probably on her way home, probably passed him while he was on his way here.'

'My daughter,' said Hinde. 'Laura. She hasn't come back.'

7

It was hard to get Hinde to speak rationally. He had come rushing here to demand of Bronwen where her husband was and when on earth he was due back, and now wanted to be rushing off somewhere else — anywhere, so long as he was on the move, hurrying through the night rather than staying still and impotent. He marched up and down the carpet as he had been doing for the ten minutes before Caspian's return, reproaching himself and abjectly pleading for Caspian's help again.

'She insisted on driving Mrs. Relph home — or Mrs. Relph insisted on it. And she ought to have returned at once, but she's still away, at this hour of the night.'

'She could have lost her way back,' Bronwen said gently, 'while you've been driving here she — '

'I should never have let her go. I see that now. Never.'

Caspian said: 'Some small mishap

could have delayed her: a damaged wheel, her horse going lame — some commonplace thing.'

'Word would surely have been sent to me.'

No soothing argument was going to satisfy Hinde.

'Where does Mrs. Relph live?' asked Caspian.

'She told us she had rooms in Bayswater, sufficient for herself and her maid. She promised before leaving to let me have the full address. But there's no sign of it. My house is as if she had never set foot in it.'

'It makes little sense.' Caspian tired, leaned against the back of Bronwen's chair. 'I thought Laura was clear of the danger period. Unless I've guessed it quite wrong.'

'If you're any good at guessing, sir, then please tell me how we may guess our way to my daughter.'

'So soon after Elaine Mancroft's death,' Caspian mused, 'perhaps they had to have a meeting. To choose . . . ' He stopped himself.

'Choose what?' demanded Hinde.

Bronwen felt the rub of her husband's mind against hers, and knew what he feared. With Elaine Mancroft gone, they must choose the next.

But why Laura, when Caspian had thought her out of danger?

Hinde said wretchedly: 'I trusted her.' They knew who he meant. 'I was too ready to be charmed by her.' He swung towards Caspian. 'Who *is* she? What part does she play in all this?'

They drove from Cheyne Walk up through Kensington and on into Bayswater. It was a clear night. The long white terraces ran into one another like the stucco façade of an endless palace. As the horses' hoofs clattered in and out of the imposing squares they struck echoes from the tall, sleeping mansions. Caspian and Bronwen sat still, silent, trying to catch other echoes. Through the clash and clatter of other minds they sought a secretive inner voice they would recognize as Elizabeth Relph's. A deep groundswell of sleep rolled over them and ebbed. Bronwen's head throbbed with the pain of it. Communication with slumbering minds was always more direct; but more confusing. In sleep, muscles and breathing and all the physical tensions of the active body were relaxed, and the mind ceased to calculate and control, and went wandering off into fantasy — or into a more colourful reality. Messages of dream and delirium pounded into Bronwen's mind. She kept mentally close to Caspian, needing his strength, clinging to him as they tried to reach through pandemonium to a clear, identifiable Elizabeth Relph.

'Damn it, what are you doing?'

To Hinde they must have appeared as two dummies, their gazes transfixed.

His impatient demand brought them back from the clamour. The quest was doomed to failure. A dog seeking one quarry through ten thousand conflicting scents stood a better chance than they did.

Caspian mopped his brow. Bronwen sank back, her head jangling, and put her hands to her ears. Caspian leaned forward. His fingertips were on her temples, he was massaging her gently, so that the ache behind her eyes faded, and with it the discord in her ears. And his mind stroked hers, calming it, so that she murmured silently, almost purred.

'We're simply wasting time,' growled Hinde.

'Yes,' said Caspian equably.

'We could enquire at the police station. Someone recently come into the neighbourhood from India might be noticed by some observant officer.'

But the police kept no records of people moving in and out of rented rooms, unless they were known wrongdoers. Mrs. Relph did not fit into that category — not in any officially identifiable way.

'In the morning,' said Bronwen, 'the Post Office may know.'

'In the morning,' said Hinde despairingly.

Caspian said: 'We really must go back to your house. There may be something there you've overlooked. Something my wife and I may respond to. And if there have been any messages, they'll be waiting for you.'

Now, veering wildly in this direction, Hinde could not wait to get home. He sat crouched forward on his seat, his mouth working, as if wanting to shout at his coachman and increase the speed beyond all reasonable bounds.

Through silent streets they sped. An occasional figure on the pavement turned to watch them go. Some late revellers leaned out of a hired omnibus to call vague greetings or abuse. The journey was accomplished in a quarter of the time it would have taken in daytime traffic.

They swept up the drive of Nasmyth Lodge. There was a light on in Laura's window; and one in the small drawing room beside the front door.

Hinde rushed unceremoniously in, not even waiting to hand Bronwen down from his carriage and up the three steps of the portico. Caspian took her arm, and they followed.

The drawing room door was half open. Sitting facing it, as if to keep watch for anyone coming in, was Elizabeth Relph. But she did not see them: she was slumped against the arm of the chair, sound asleep.

Hinde stood petrified for a moment.

They could not see his face, but saw the hunching of his shoulders and the clasping and spasmodic unclasping of his right fist.

Mrs. Relph gave a start, and woke up.

She looked into Hinde's face. 'I brought her back. She's safe.'

'But why wasn't she home sooner — why couldn't she come back on her own?'

'She's safe.' Mrs. Relph appeared utterly exhausted. Her tongue slurred the words and she gave every sign of collapsing into sleep again.

Hinde turned uncertainly towards the door. 'Laura?'

'I locked her in her room . . . in case she attempted to . . . to answer the summons herself.'

As Hinde hurried up the wide staircase, Bronwen and Caspian instinctively moved closer, standing one to either side of Elizabeth Relph. Her eyelids were drooping. Caspian stared until her head turned towards him and she made herself stare back. Bronwen sensed that she knew what would be asked of her, and was fatalistically ready with the answers.

Caspian said: 'You took her to a group meeting.'

'No.'

'You were sent here to win Laura's confidence and reclaim her.'

'That part of it is true, yes.'

'And this evening you took her to a pre-arranged ceremony following up the death of one of your members, Elaine Mancroft.'

'Yes, that was the plan. But I didn't carry it through. I brought her home.'

'Brought her home when you'd finished the ritual. What was planted in her mind?' Inexorably Caspian said: 'What is Ilona to her — and to you?'

'I've never heard the name.'

'Has Laura brought Ilona back within her?'

'I pray,' said Elizabeth Relph with searing fervour, 'that she has brought nothing. That she's left with nothing of the past, and has caught nothing. From me or anyone. She suffered no harm at the meeting because she did not go.'

'You admit you set out with the

intention of luring Miss Hinde — '

'Dr. Caspian!' Hinde stood in the doorway. 'I'll not have Mrs. Relph harried in such fashion in my house.'

Without taking his eyes off the woman, Caspian said: 'Only a short time ago, sir, you were convinced you'd made a fatal misjudgment about Mrs. Relph.'

'I owe her an apology for thinking so. Seeing her, I can no longer believe such unworthy things.'

'Quite a spell you cast, ma'am.' Caspian took a deep breath. 'Will you now tell Mr. Hinde what you've just told us?' When there was no answer he insisted: 'You came to this house to recapture Laura.'

'Yes.'

'Contriving an accident, or taking advantage of the accident, you insinuated yourself into this household.'

'Yes.'

'And tonight it was your duty to accompany Laura to a preordained ritual.'

'Yes.'

Hinde let out the sob of a small, hurt child.

'You took her to this ceremony, and — '

'No.' Tears began to form from the deep pools of her eyes. 'I've told you. I didn't take her.'

'You spirited her from this house at the chosen time. Where did you go?'

'To my rooms, as planned. And there we sat until it was time to go.'

'To the meeting.'

Mrs. Relph nodded. 'But we did not go. Laura wanted to: she felt it, knew the time had come, and wanted to be there. I had to ... to struggle with her.' She wiped a hand across her eyes. 'I fought with her — yes, fought with her — until I was sure it was too late for us to leave. And then, when I had tired her out, I brought her home.'

Hinde was trying to say something, but no sound would come.

Bronwen said gently: 'What made you change your mind?'

'And defy your instructions,' Caspian added.

For the first time Mrs. Relph avoided his gaze. 'Something I've known little enough of, until now.'

They waited.

She raised her eyes again, and said: 'Love.'

'Love — for Laura?'

'For Laura, yes. And' — it was little more than a whisper, but true and steady — 'for her father.'

★　★　★

The street was one of six, running parallel, each named after a great battle in British history — battles which had ended in British victories — but each looking private and decorous rather than warlike. Coloured glass panels in the front doors were like a series of secular church windows.

Number 15 Vimeiro Road had a front step scrubbed to match its neighbours, and a letterbox flap that gleamed from repeated polishing.

Caspian knocked twice.

Within the house a door slammed. Footsteps scurried along the passage. A little girl in black bombazine, with a starched white cap and apron, opened the door and peered up awestruck into

Caspian's beard.

He said: 'Is Mrs. Garston at home?'

'Yes, sir. I mean, I'll go and see. What name would it be, sir?'

'Caspian. Dr. Alexander Caspian.'

She was back in a rustle of skirt and apron, holding the door back a few more inches. 'This way, sir. The mistress will — er — receive you.'

He was shown into a parlour hung with coloured views of mountains, a child's embroidered sampler, cameos of the Queen and her late Prince Consort, overshadowed by a large reproduction of *The Monarch of the Glen*. Candle-holders on the upright piano were as bright as the letterbox outside.

Mrs. Garston was a thin woman of faded prettiness, very trim, her manner tightly laced as though she had learned to enjoy the discomfort of it.

'There must be a mistake,' she said. 'I haven't sent for any doctor.'

'Mrs. Garston, I don't want to revive too many unhappy memories, but I'd be most grateful if you could tell me a few things about your late husband.'

'Everything's settled: the Friendly Society, the debts cleared up, there's not a penny outstanding.'

'I'm sure there isn't.'

'Then what . . . ?'

Remembering her prim etiquette suddenly, she indicated that her visitor should seat himself in a high-backed chair set at right angles to the fireplace. She settled herself in a facing chair.

Caspian said: 'At the inquest you said he went out for a walk, although the fog would be injurious to his health.'

'I did, yes.'

'And that he was following some medical treatment other than that recommended by your usual doctor.'

One arm rose protectively across her narrow bosom. 'It wasn't you? It wouldn't have been you he went to see?'

'I'm not a doctor of medicine, but of philosophy.'

'Philosophy?' She permitted herself a bleak smile. 'I've needed plenty of that in my time.'

'This medical treatment of his — '

'That's what he made out it was,

though I had my doubts.'

'What course did he have to follow and what effect did it have on him?'

Suspicion pricked her lips. 'Why are you so interested? It's over, he's gone, he's dead. I told the coroner all I knew. No sense in dragging it all up again.'

'There are others who may have been involved in the same group. I want to save them, if I can, from going the same way.'

She struggled with this. After a few moments she said grudgingly: 'I never saw any sign of it doing him any good at all. But something kept driving him on,'

'From the records of his death' — Caspian did not propose to alarm her by mentioning that it was the police who had so swiftly and efficiently supplied these records — 'I gather his birthday was the 10th of March, and he died a week after that.'

'It wasn't much of a birthday. The children made a fuss of him, and he got too excited and had one of his attacks. Leaving me to clean up and try to keep them happy.'

'He suffered a great deal?'

'Our own doctor said he hadn't long to live.' It came out sharp and angry. 'They wanted him in hospital but didn't hold out much hope, and he said he'd do things his own way and he'd show them a thing or two. There was this somebody else he'd never describe to me, and something he never explained properly but kept boasting about in the strangest roundabout way. It was going to cure him. It *had* to. He was going to insist, before it was too late.' She snorted a dour laugh. 'Doctor, what do you think they did to him — or could have done for him?'

'Made him believe that he was going to get better,' said Caspian. It sounded too glib and too uncomplicated.

'But he didn't get better.'

Caspian saw that the widow was fidgeting again and was about to ask him again about the reason for his presence. He anticipated her: 'Where did he go for these consultations?'

'The first couple of times he said it was in lecture rooms, somewhere over in Camden Town. Then he grew secretive. All he'd say was that he was one of those specially chosen for treatment, and there was going to be a great change, and it was something I wouldn't understand. He kept it all to himself, except every now and then he'd say he was going to outlive us all.'

'Was there any set times for these meetings?'

'If there was, he never said a word in advance. He'd just tell me on his way out. You'd have thought he'd forgotten until the last minute, and then suddenly it'd come to him — as if someone had come to the door to call for him, and he'd be up and off. And there was no arguing with him.'

'The place where he . . . met with his accident . . . drowned. Would that have been on the way to another rendezvous?'

He thought of the item in the records, insignificant in police eyes but by a stroke of good fortune and meticulous observation noted down: the missing fingernail ('Probably torn off when he was trying to pull himself out') and the patch on his scalp from which hair had been torn ('Might have got caught in the landing-stage, holding him down long enough to drown before he pulled away').

Mrs. Garston said: 'He was especially anxious to be on his way that night. The time before, he'd come back even more out of sorts than usual, and said he was being kept waiting and it couldn't go on. This last time, he was — well, desperate.' Her arm dropped until her hand lay limp on her knee. 'Said he'd outlive us all!' She sounded too disillusioned for there to be either humour or spitefulness in the echo.

The candleholders on the piano caught a shaft of sunlight as Caspian rose to take his leave.

★   ★   ★

His hands found sombre chords and modulated up to meet the loving lament of her song. She improvised an eerie cadenza, something stolen from the Welsh hills, and he picked her up on a long trill and carried her into another key, from which she escaped down a long chromatic descent into a stream of Cymric melancholy.

They needed no written music and no

rehearsal. In every sense they were in tune. When Bronwen sang, he was not playing an accompaniment but creating the song with her as they went along; until he raised his hands from the keyboard and spun round on the stool. 'No, you've gone too far. There are no such notes on the pianoforte.'

'So much the worse for the pianoforte.'

In the depths of the house the doorbell tinkled faintly.

'Our guests.' Caspian got up from the stool. 'Let's hope that this time they'll be capable of fitting in some of the missing pieces.'

Joseph Hinde watched fondly as his daughter and Mrs. Relph settled side by side on a long window stool. 'They've both slept for the better part of a day and a half,' he confided. 'I wouldn't have disturbed them for the world.' And then, accusingly: 'And I'll not have you disturb them too much now. I agree to just one more attempt to get to the bottom of this business: against my better judgment, but Laura wants to get it out of her system.'

With which he accepted the chair

Bronwen had offered him, looking from one to another of them as if presiding over a committee.

Caspian, too, looked from face to face: from Laura Hinde to Elizabeth Relph. Bronwen felt a totally unexpected tug of jealousy. Intuitively she sensed Caspian's response to Elizabeth. The woman's spell was powerful. It was pure, untrammeled, sensual womanhood. Pure — an odd word, yet the only possible one. Hinde had succumbed to her spell; and succumbed a second time.

Keeping his voice level, Caspian said: 'Mrs. Relph, perhaps you'll begin. Tell us what you remember about your own part in the group, and about Laura's introduction to it.'

'I remember nothing. It's all gone,' said Elizabeth. 'There's this odd ache, and that's all: like the pain in my knee after the accident, dying away and then stopping altogether.'

Caspian turned to Laura. 'And you?'

Two little furrows creased her brow. 'Elizabeth's right. Just this ache, fading away.'

'Ilona. When did you last speak to Ilona?'

'You've used that name before. Who is she?'

'You don't recall anything about her?'

They both shook their heads like demure schoolgirls.

'You're sure?'

Bronwen moved mentally up beside Caspian, waiting for the faintest tremor of flesh excited by flesh, for some echo of that all-consuming greed. They listened for that other voice.

It was not there. No resonance, no reply.

Everything had been stilled on the sounding board of memory. If Ilona had indeed been more than a manifestation of Laura's hidden conflicts, she was gone now. Laura and Elizabeth had disobeyed the summons to the ritual, and so all tell-tale recollections had been muted.

'Well, that's the end of that,' said Hinde with some satisfaction.

'With these ladies' permission,' said Caspian, 'and with their help, I want to continue the investigation.'

'They're safe. It's over.'

'So you thought before.' Caspian turned back to Laura. 'Miss Hinde, you resisted mesmerism once before. Would you be prepared to co-operate this time?'

She hesitated; then nodded.

As Hinde was about to protest, Caspian went on: 'I shall be happy for Mrs. Relph to be present. And my wife.'

They went to his study. It was sparsely furnished, the walls washed a deep olive green, with no picture or mirror or ornament to distract the attention. There were four chairs, one of them an upholstered armchair with a long sloping back. He guided Laura to this and nudged a footstool into place. When her feet were on it, he sat at the extreme end of the stool and looked into her eyes. Elizabeth drew an upright chair closer. Bronwen settled herself behind Caspian.

'Is there anything I can hope to reveal?' Laura wondered aloud.

'There'll be traces,' he assured her. 'Something in your consciousness has obeyed an instruction to expunge certain selected memories. But somewhere in there some traces must remain.'

He began to talk in a musical rhythm, lulling her with words, which rang tunefully but meant nothing. At the same time his hand moved to and fro before her eyes as if conducting a slow, lilting movement of a symphony.

Words came. 'You are at a meeting, Laura. In the usual place.'

Her eyes had glazed over. Perhaps, fractionally, she nodded.

'The usual place. You know how to get there?'

'The chapel,' she said. There was a pause. Bronwen felt herself keeping step with Laura, trudging up a short hill to where a dark building stood back from its neighbours in shadow. The distance shortened, and without being aware of opening any door they were inside.

Caspian's voice was leading rein, guiding his mind and Bronwen's in upon Laura.

'They are all present, aren't they?'

'She is there. In the pulpit, as usual.'

Her answers were dredged painfully up from muddied depths. At the same time Bronwen and Caspian responded to other resonances, sketching in, then smearing, the background to those spoken replies. In one vivid moment they were in the chapel with Laura, and the veiled woman was leaning out from her shadowy pulpit.

Elizabeth nodded to herself; the slow swing of question and answer appeared to have awoken her own vague recollections.

Caspian said: 'Laura — what part did you yourself play in the ritual?'

'I . . . ' The sound became a sigh, and trailed away. Bronwen and Caspian reached in to keep a grip on Laura, while he said urgently: 'You had a special part to play. A special purpose in being there. You will tell me.'

'I . . . ' Again she was slipping away, further away. Then, plaintively: 'I was waiting.'

'For what?'

'When the chosen ones had gone through, in turn . . . '

They had an awareness of dwindling numbers, of a select few growing fewer, moving on and moving through.

'When were the choices made, and how?'

'I was not told. I was not one of them.'

Bronwen felt the puzzlement in her husband's mind. 'Not one of them? But you joined the group, you were selected, you were among the ones chosen to continue.' He shot it at her: 'Weren't you the fire symbol?'

'Fire?' It had no meaning for her.

'Your birth date must mean what I think it means. It's got to be the fire element.' His confusion confused Laura, too, and again she slid through his grasp. 'What promise was made to you?' he demanded.

'I wasn't one of those chosen to go through.'

'Nor I,' Elizabeth added.

'Then why were you there, the two of you?'

A familiar sadness flooded up from Laura like the rising level of a sombre, unplumbed well. A woman's face emerged from the shades. Bronwen's pulse quickened as she sought to define the lineaments of the woman in the pulpit. Would it, this time, be the stab of an accusation or the invitation of those warm, sensuous arms?

The face became clearer. Now Bronwen realized there was only one person it could be.

'Mother,' whispered Laura.

She had gone to the Camden Lecture Rooms after trying, without her father's knowledge, other séances and other abortive meetings. Mr. Hinde had business and Parliamentary duties to occupy him. She, spared only a few cold minutes of his time, sought the lost, loving companionship of her mother.

'It was promised,' she said.

'By whom?'

'By her.'

'What did she promise?'

'All I had to do was be patient, and wait until all the other elements fell into place.'

'Elements?'

Bronwen sought to clutch the elusive thought behind Laura's uncertainties, but already it was obscured.

Caspian went on: 'Were any of you asked to make a pact with the Devil?'

On this at any rate she was certain: firm in denial.

'Might it have been asked of those who 'went through', as you put it?'

Both Laura and Elizabeth exuded a fleeting, shared fear of that veiled creature who scurried along the fringe of consciousness like someone brushing against the far side of a velvet curtain, moulding it to freakish shapes and then dodging away. Then all at once Laura's eyes began to clear. She was waking of her own accord, without waiting for Caspian's command.

'The address of the chapel?' he implored, striving to hold her. 'The street it's in — quickly!'

He was too late. Some will of her own rejected him; and not only him. Once and for all both the veiled figure and that naked, possessive body which had tempted her were dismissed in a silent cry of shame. It was not the veiled woman discarding an unworthy disciple, but Laura finally dismissing every last trace of the woman.

'You?' Caspian swung towards Elizabeth. 'The street — you remember that much? If we could find the meeting place, if . . . '

She shook her head. 'There's nothing left.'

'Why did you join the group?'

'There's nothing left,' she repeated.

Laura was staring innocently at Caspian, waiting to be told whether she had been a good and helpful girl or whether things were just as before.

He said: 'Somewhere I must have misinterpreted something. The gap where the fire sign should have come . . . no, I don't understand. Basically I'm sure of what it means, what it has to mean. But the gaps . . . ' Bronwen shared with him a picture which might well have been a painting by Hieronymus Bosch: a wide canvas of flickering colour and, from a distance, of unidentifiable spots and twisted shapes, but then revealing under close examination some grotesque imp skulking in every cranny. 'You were being used,' he declared, 'or at least it was the intention to use you, in a symbolic transmutation of elements.'

Laura and Elizabeth exchanged baffled glances.

'I'm talking about alchemy. That's what it's about. And, from all you say, that most unnatural of practitioners: a woman alchemist. What I'm not clear about is what she has been striving to create.' He clapped his hands loudly together, as he had done on stage if an assistant was a fraction of a second late on a cue. 'It's like some exasperating party game — a charade, with some essential syllables still missing.'

8

Talk of séances and spiritualism had been bad enough. The idea of alchemy was altogether too much. Joseph Hinde watched a leisurely curl of blue smoke from one of Caspian's best Havanas. His tightening lips looked ready to bite the end off it.

'First the evil eye, then mesmerism, and now we're round a charlatan's fire brewing up gold. Is there no end to this abracadabra?'

Bronwen poured tea. Laura and Elizabeth had resumed their places on the window stool. Stirring the tea in their cups, they made a genteel picture against which that of ancient wizards churning macabre mixtures in cauldrons did indeed seem incongruous.

Caspian said: 'Let's forget the abracadabra. Alchemy always aspired to be more than that: far, far more than a greed for wealth. The alchemists sought first to refine their own consciousness; and on the way found parallels in the physical world. The base metals they brought together for conversion into gold represented, first and foremost, the elements and energies of human nature: the gold symbolizes the attainment of spiritual knowledge and the purity of true immortality.'

'I consulted you, Doctor, in the hope of your knocking some of the nonsense out of my daughter's head. I didn't realize you accepted a good half of that nonsense yourself.'

'It's hard to find an effective way of defeating an enemy if you don't first accept that enemy's existence.'

'These discredited heresies — '

'For good or ill, many of your so-called heresies were active before the orthodoxies. Our present religions and sciences haven't succeeded in ousting them.'

Bronwen knew with chilling certainty that Caspian had committed himself now. They were not dealing with one imbalanced girl's foibles or even with the dabblings of a group of mere eccentrics.

Caspian had made it clear that he acknowledged the existence of a real opponent. Fashioned out of what ill-will and ancient greed?

Hinde had not been tried in such terrors as Bronwen and Caspian had known, and she would not have wished to subject any fellow human being to the ordeal. But to those unscathed it was hard to explain the thousand and one complexities of worlds interwoven with our own.

'Alchemist and adept,' Caspian went on, 'worked to the same principle. *Solve et coagula*: dissolve and combine. Base metal must be 'killed' by stripping away all its false characteristics. With the dross eliminated, the true metal could shine through to a new life and be imbued with more desirable characteristics. So with the spirit of man: the killing of the metal represents the ritual death of initiation into the great Mysteries and emergence into new life.'

'You can't believe that in our modem society — '

'It's not what I believe, but what the

199

practitioners believe. Without belief no formula will work. That was always held to be true, and still is.'

'All the belief in the world won't produce gold from heaps of scrap metal, or turn a base mind into a noble one.'

'No salvation for those who repent their sins? A harsh judgment. And even in this everyday world, look at what our minds are capable of. Charcot has established at the Salpetriere that mere ideas can produce physical changes. Hysteria is of psychical origin. Good or ill health can be governed by the will — in other words, sheer belief can cause actual biological and chemical changes. Is there any reason to suppose the process has to stop there?'

'Simply by taking thought we shall cleanse ourselves of impurities, add a cubit to our stature, control disease, choose how to live and when to die?'

In his scorn Hinde found it convenient to forget his own fear that simply by taking thought his daughter had seemed to will herself towards death.

Caspian said: 'For two centuries the

scientific world has concerned itself only with what it can touch and handle and weigh, and we've uncritically accepted Boyle's supposed demolition of Aristotelian theory. Laboratories have abandoned any attempt to convert one element into another. But if taken in the right sequence, at the right speed, in the right conditions . . . '

'You'll be handing out the recipe for the Philosopher's Stone any moment now.'

'What do our most up-to-date scientists believe in, if not in that? They are turning back, at last, to the practice of alchemy — confident that the solution to the mystery of creation itself is at their fingertips. Their etheric theories have new names, but any alchemist would know what they are preaching. This particle known as the atom is no more or less than the 'first matter' of Hermes Trismegistus, the seed of all potential life and phenomena. At the moment there is too much concern with material applications. But here and there are inheritors of the old tradition, those who have never forgotten the psychical parallel and continue to work along it — for good,' said Caspian gravely, 'or ill.'

'I still fail to see what all this has to do with Laura's temporary aberration.'

Hinde did not really wish to see. For their part, Laura and Elizabeth sat with cups and saucers delicately poised, polite and attentive but somehow no longer a part of what had happened or nearly happened to them.

Caspian said: 'Very well. Let's consider the personal application. Like most mystical rites, alchemy derives its formulae from the relationship of the four elements and the twelve signs of the zodiac. According to the adepts we are all compounded of earth, air, fire and water; and the predominance of one or other of those elements in our character is itself governed by our birth sign, and that in turn by astral conjunctions and ascendancies at the time of our birth. By now I'm convinced' — he leaned forward to stress the words and jolt the three from their polite indifference — 'that the group which Mrs. Relph and Miss Hinde were persuaded to join was fashioned around a sequence of birth signs, each related to a successive element. At the earliest meeting, were you asked for the date and time of your birth?'

Mrs. Relph looked doubtful. 'I . . . there were some ordinary questions . . . no, I can't be sure.'

'I seem to remember,' said Laura. Then: 'Yes, because there was something about age, and where we were born . . . not much was made of it, but we were asked something. It didn't seem important.'

'But it was most important. The whole preliminary selection procedure must have been based on it. Let's see . . . A man or woman born between the 19th of February and the 20th of March is subject to the governance of Pisces and the element of water. Such people are most susceptible to characteristic inborn humours and to outside influences during the period when Pisces is dominant; and within that period a man will be most truly himself, a woman most truly herself, when the planets ruling at their birth are again in the ascendancy, with Sun or

Moon in their most powerful aspects. The Sun in Pisces is said to create depression and anxiety. Mercury and Neptune in conjunction will provoke changeable moods and an almost inevitable sorrow. One man under such influences was a member of your group and died in his governing element, water, at the beginning of the sequence.

'You, Miss Hinde, were born on the 24th of March. That is, you are an Aries subject and your element is fire. I don't know what was planned for you — voluntary immolation by fire seems to fit the pattern — but thanks to your father's intervention and then, even more significantly, to Mrs. Relph's change of heart, you've been spared. Frankly I'd have expected such a break in the sequence to throw the calculations out, so that the ritual would have to begin all over again. But since the water subject died right at the end of the relevant period, and the earth subject close to the beginning of hers, the adept — your veiled priestess who has now sought to wipe herself from your minds, ladies — is perhaps hoping to complete the cycle without it being too seriously unbalanced by that gap, and to add a fire subject at the end with someone born under Leo.'

Elizabeth Relph's interest seemed to have been aroused more than that of the others. 'You spoke of an earth subject,' she said curiously.

'Elaine Mancroft, the actress, died in the earth of a partially opened grave. She fits the pattern remarkably. Or not so remarkably. Predictably, rather — if one had been in time to make such a prediction and possibly avert its consequences. Her ruling planet was Venus, and the fifth House was controlled by Virgo and Mercury — a conjunction predicating a number of lovers, a wayward personality, and violent swings of fortune.'

'With you in the field, Mr. Rider Haggard will have to look to his laurels.' Hinde waved away Bronwen's offer of another cup of tea.

'Next,' Caspian persevered, 'comes an air sign: a Gemini subject between the 21st of May and the 21st of June.' Hinde made a show of being too contemptuous to listen further, but started when Caspian added: 'Sir Andrew Thornhill comes within those degrees. It would be interesting to consult an ephemeris and see at what date there might be a conjunction of factors similar to those prevailing at his birth.'

'An ephemeris?'

'An astronomical almanac. It shows the computed positions of the major heavenly bodies over any given period.'

Hinde got grumpily to his feet. Laura dutifully followed suit. Elizabeth Relph let her attention linger a moment longer on Caspian, then smiled apologetically and passed her cup and saucer to Bronwen.

'Before I go,' said Hinde heavily, 'will you tell us, Doctor, what this sequence of yours is supposed to lead up to, and what it's got to do with alchemy, and what it's got to do with Thornhill and my daughter?'

Caspian stood beside Elizabeth Relph. Her head came to his shoulder. She moved slightly round from the window so that she was standing in his shadow, and she was still smiling — a slightly puzzled smile now, as if something obscure stirred in the back of her mind.

He said: 'Each of the people involved represents one of the four elements essential for alchemy: water, fire, air and earth. Two are dead, two still mercifully alive. When all four have . . . played their part . . . from them would be fashioned whatever it is the alchemist wishes to fashion.'

'And my part?' asked Elizabeth. 'My birthday's in early September. A long way ahead.'

'The catalytic ingredient! What else? The essential addition of the elixir which releases the essence of all the others!'

Hinde moved possessively to Elizabeth's other side. 'So you are the Philosopher's Stone, my dear?' He took her arm. 'Not that that surprises me. And my brother-in-law a figure of air? Hum, yes.' He laughed. 'Apt enough.'

Thornhill. *I want to live to see it . . . our new knowledge.*

Bronwen and Caspian heard another echo, that of Daniel Clegg speaking of Elaine: *She wants to be immortal because she daren't die.*

Hinde escorted Elizabeth down the path to the gate as his carriage was brought up. Laura paused under the shade of the plane tree beside the path. Caspian said: 'Miss Hinde, when you were trying to reach your mother and ultimately answered that advertisement, did you have any idea of seeking immortality with her: death, and reunion in the world beyond?'

'Oh, no.' Laura contemplated the recent past as if over a great distance. 'All I remember is wanting to talk to Mother and not be lonely, and hear she was still alive and happy somewhere.'

'And you don't remember what was asked from you in return?'

She moved out of the shade to rejoin her father. 'It's all gone for good. It was morbid, I can see that now. I won't be so silly again.'

With farewell handshakes at the gate, Hinde said: 'Sorry my girl hasn't been much help. But I think we agreed this was to be the end of it?' Stiffly and with little conviction he added: 'I'm grateful for all you've done.'

'Done?' said Caspian to Bronwen as he

turned back up the path. 'We haven't done half enough. The thing isn't by any means safely over. The working of the ritual has still to be completed.'

'Without Laura? And, if you're right in identifying Mrs. Relph as the catalytic element, without her also?'

'I don't know. Damn it, we don't know nearly enough.'

Indoors he sat at the pianoforte but for once derived no consolation from it. He shut the lid. Bronwen rang for the tray to be taken away. When they were alone together she said: 'Neither of them retains any memory of getting to the meeting-place, or of how they knew the exact time to go. Did that drowned man's widow have anything to say about it? Or Clegg?'

Caspian thought back over the two interviews. 'I got the impression both victims were suddenly reminded. It could hardly have been done by letter: in Laura's case, Hinde might have noticed it and intercepted it, and something like that could have applied to the others as well.'

'By telepathy, then?'

'We two know how difficult the most

carefully calculated message is to transmit, even between people attuned like ourselves. I can't credit such communication over wide gaps between disparate people. It seems more feasible that in each ritual a summons to the next gathering would be mesmerically implanted.'

'Like an alarm clock.'

'Exactly.'

They sat in silence for a while, recognizing the necessity of establishing the correct rhythm for the strange dance in which they were still involved. The mathematical music of the zodiac was an essential part of the ritual: not just the ground bass and harmony of its governing elements, but the rhythm binding it all together.

From the hypnotic dances of pagan tribes to the formalities of the Mass, through the brisk pulse of evangelical hymns to the protracted orders of service for every festival and every penance, through every seasonal ceremony and private incantation, there had to be a prevailing pace that would discipline all else. Implanted in the minds of the group to which Thornhill, Laura,

Elaine Mancroft and Henry Garston had each added a personal note there must indeed have been a certain note set for a certain time, a bell to call them to worship or to certain preordained actions at an appointed place.

Bronwen broke the silence. 'So we have the four elements and we have the alchemist, the veiled woman. In addition, Mrs. Relph may have been selected as the activating salt to liberate fire, air, earth and water into a new creation. But what's it to be, this new creation?'

Said he'd outlive the rest of us.

'The Philosopher's Stone,' said Caspian reflectively. 'The Elixir of Life. The goal of every alchemist's quest. But of course.' His head came up, his eyes were bright. 'Immortality!'

'That's what you were asking Laura Hinde about.'

'But I'd got it wrong way round. I was thinking in terms of some mutual suicide, somehow compacted with a promise of happiness beyond — release from pain, meeting with loved ones, eternal bliss. But it's not that at all, is it?'

'That advertisement.' She caught the gesture of his thoughts. 'It offered eternity in this world.'

'Of course it did. Immortality here on earth: that was what Garston wanted. And Elaine Mancroft too. After suitable ritual preparation, and under a mesmeric spell, they'd go willingly into the ordeal from which they expected to emerge renewed. Such alchemy works only if the elements surrender their essence of their own free will: it cannot be beaten out of them with mallets and chisels and presses. Immortality,' he breathed, 'in this world, on this plane.'

'But so far two of the elements have proved mortal, and have perished.'

'Or will be transmuted when the other two sacrifices are completed.'

'You see them as sacrifices?'

'At first I thought of some communal rite in which they were all equals. But obviously they're all subordinate to that damned woman — '

'Damned,' said Bronwen. It throbbed away into infinity.

He tugged at his beard. 'But Laura

wasn't looking for personal immortality. Not for herself. Somewhere I made some false assumption about her relationship to the fire element. It doesn't fit. But as for the rest, what have we got? A handful of gullible fools tempted by the oldest of all Mephistophelian trickeries in return for their contribution to . . . well, to what?'

'Immortality.'

'We've already established that two were driven to suicide. A fine sort of — '

'*Her* immortality,' said Bronwen. 'The woman who brought them together. We've heard her, and she can have meant only one thing: drawing from others the vitality for her own renewal.'

'Lilith. And Salome.'

'And Ilona.'

No, this time it will be different.

'We must reach that woman,' said Caspian, 'before she attains the consummation of her ritual.'

'Will it work? Even according to the celebrant's own theories, I mean? There ought surely to be simultaneous mingling of the elements and the catalytic elixir in one place at one time, not spread over a period as this seems to have been.'

'The hair,' he reminded her. 'The nails. Torn from that fellow Garston. And from Elaine Mancroft. An ancient sorcery, boding no good to the victims. Provided death comes about when the planetary juxtapositions are in their most significant aspects, the hair and nail parings will retain their vital qualities until the time comes to blend them.'

'And Sir Andrew Thornhill is next.'

'If our reckoning is correct.'

'Is there no way of warning him?'

'I don't fancy trying to break the news to him,' said Caspian ruefully. 'After that last occasion I doubt if he'd be in a receptive mood.'

'But we can't just let him walk into . . . into whatever it is.'

* * *

This part of the problem, if no other, was unexpectedly eased by an invitation, which arrived two weeks later. Mr. Joseph Hinde requested the pleasure of their company at dinner at Nasmyth Lodge on the 25th of May. His letter, written in a fine regular hand, said that he would have a personal announcement of the greatest significance to make, and in view of their own part in the matter he particularly wished them to be present.

'His daughter's intending to marry?' suggested Caspian.

'Or he is.'

They accepted the invitation, and arrived as requested at six o'clock on that Friday afternoon; finding to their surprise that, in spite of Hinde's previous strictures about his brother-in law and his outburst in the Pantheon Club, Sir Andrew was also among the guests.

9

Spring was flowering into summer. Light showers had freshened the grass, sharpening the contrast between green lawns and the sunny brightness of red brick and white stucco. Joseph Hinde stood on his terrace and wondered if there could ever be a future day to match this one.

His empty world was suddenly populated — though all the figures in it were just reflections of one person. Wherever he looked this warm, still evening, he caught the quiver of flowered muslin and the twist of a smile; was aware of her talking to Dr. Caspian and then, while he engaged the Dampiers in conversation, laughing with Laura. There was a double pleasure in that: she and Laura, belonging together.

Far above his head there was the rattle of a window catch. Hinde looked up. His brother-in-law had come out through one of the second-floor casement windows on to the balcony, which ran the length of the southern façade, commanding a long vista of gardens, the curving reaches of the Thames, and meadows and mansions beyond.

'All the kingdoms of the earth!' Thornhill leaned on the low balustrade. 'Must make you feel very lordly and remote when you're up here, Joseph.'

Remote, yes, but he had never consciously wished to lord it over anyone. Perhaps to others he had appeared stiff and impersonal — for fear of admitting that as a person he was of no consequence.

Now he was of consequence, in a way he had never imagined, under a spell, which sent his blood coursing through his veins.

'Come on down, Andrew. I've something to tell you all.'

Not so many of them, when he looked around. When he had felt the need for a little flourish, to have friends present to hear his news, he had found how few there were who could be called friend. He had managed so long without; had lived by principle rather than people. The

Dampiers were as close as any, yet without their business association would they have anything to say to one another? Sons of the founders of the Hinde and Dampier porcelain factory, he and Simeon had assumed that their own sons would tidily continue the pattern. But Gerald was dead, and the only neat possibility now was a marriage between Robert Dampier and Laura. Many a time he had tetchily reproved her for her indifference to Robert. Now, he saw clearly that she would not be happy with such a young man. Charlotte Dampier kept pushing the two of them archly together, but she was wasting her time. He would not ask happiness for himself and condemn his daughter to something less.

'Down to earth again, eh?'

Andrew Thornhill came out on to the terrace.

Inviting Thornhill had been a matter of duty. He was, after all, Florence's brother.

And the only other guests were the Caspians. Without them, or without the circumstances in which they had become involved, he might not have met Elizabeth.

218

His heart missed a beat. If she had not been there that day, had not been injured, had not become so fond of Laura . . . and then, incredibly, of himself . . . 'Love.' He heard her voice, he would never forget the sound of those words. 'For Laura, yes. And for her father.'

He had thought of making the announcement halfway through dinner. Suddenly it became imperative that he should speak now and set the seal on it.

Thornhill had no glass. Hinde waited while the footman crossed the terrace with a silver tray.

'Well, Joseph? Going to announce that Her Majesty has sent for you and secretly asked you to form a new Government? No more Conservatives and Liberals: long life to the New Moral Party!'

Beside the sculpted granite urn, Elizabeth was talking to Mrs. Caspian. Hinde waited for her to turn her head. When their glances crossed she at once began to move towards him.

None of her own friends had come today, because she had none in England. She had lived too far away for too long.

Nobody but himself.

When they were standing side by side he raised his voice and said: 'It was kind of you all to come this evening. I have asked you here on this auspicious occasion so that I could tell you that Mrs. Relph has consented to be my wife. I consider myself a most fortunate man. Please be true friends and tell her some falsehoods about my good points — I've made a pretty poor job of doing so myself.'

Mrs. Dampier burst ecstatically into tears, as Hinde had privately predicted she would. He found it pleasing and very right and proper in the circumstances.

Laura kissed his cheek and hugged him, as she had done when he first told her of his intentions. He had felt apprehensive, remembering the deep attachment that had led her to pursue her mother even after death. But Laura had been so unfeignedly happy. Was love really such a sweet and easy solution to everything?

'Congratulations, sir.' Caspian shook hands, and bowed to Elizabeth. 'This really is the happiest resolution.'

Mrs. Dampier moved in, mopping her eyes.

Thornhill downed his drink and waved the empty glass peremptorily at the footman. 'Joseph, you old dog. Though I must say I'm a mite offended . . . Calling me down in a hurry, and pouring out this excellent champagne — I was sure you were going to wish me a happy birthday!'

'Today? My dear Andrew, I'm so sorry. With all my own selfish preoccupations — '

'No matter — you'll have many more opportunities. More,' said Thornhill ruminatively, 'than you may think.' Then he was boisterous again, reaching out an arm to trap Laura as she came within reach. 'Your daughter didn't forget, anyway, bless her. Say it again, my love, just to make sure.'

'Many happy returns of the day, Uncle Andrew.' His birthday. Of course: the 25th of May. Walking beside Elizabeth Relph, approaching the plinth of the little temple, Caspian wondered what the astral conjunctions had been on the day or night of Sir Andrew Thornhill's birth. The veiled priestess, or Ilona, or the two in one, must know; and those balances in the zodiac had dictated the choice of Thornhill. With more information, Caspian might at this moment have hurried back across the lawn to command Thornhill's attention, to warn him that perhaps tonight, perhaps within these next few days, he would be in mortal danger.

Before the evening was out he must speak with Thornhill, no matter what rebuff was offered.

'I think that would be correct, don't you?'

Elizabeth cocked her head to look up at him as they went into the shadows of the little colonnade.

'I — I'm sorry, I — '

'You're miles away,' Elizabeth smiled. 'I was saying we shall not marry until the end of the Parliamentary session. Then it will be over a year since my husband's death. I was hoping that would be thought proper.'

She stood close to the statue of the petrified goddess, the folds of her muslin dress stirring in the faintest of breezes. Caspian felt a stab of undeniable, impenitent sensuality. He had rarely experienced from any woman such a potent incense of sexual provocation, without any hint of invitation. It was not contrived, but as much a part of her as the clouded violet of her eyes and as little capable of suppression as the quizzical wrinkles in the corners of those eyes.

He said: 'Whatever the two of you decide to do, I'm confident it will come out right.'

'I've seen your wife look at you sometimes,' she said unexpectedly, 'and yet she isn't really looking at you. In some way you know. And there's a way you . . . go very still, and somehow you're together.' She touched the ribbon in the looped plait of her hair, and she might have been touching the side of his head, trying to listen to him, through her fingertips. 'I'd like to believe it can be like that for Joseph and myself.'

Caspian tried the iron handle of the temple door, which opened before him.

'Isn't this usually locked?'

'I don't know.'

They went into the stark yet elegant interior of what, this evening, had become a cool summerhouse, with a gracefully domed ceiling. Two narrow lancet windows let in shafts of light, disturbed by shadows of leaves and branches swaying across them. In the centre of the tessellated floor was an incongruous beechwood armchair, facing the door.

'Does Mr. Hinde come here to write his speeches?'

'I haven't asked him,' said Elizabeth. 'It's another of the many things I don't know.'

Automatically they moved round the back of the chair to see what its occupant would see if he raised his head. Framed in the opening of the doorway was a dazzling segment of the lawn and the jagged outline of the urn at the end of the terrace. Joseph Hinde stepped into view, talking to someone hidden by the door itself. Then he stepped out of sight. Bronwen and Sir Andrew Thornhill crossed the bright patch and disappeared in their turn.

'I hope I'm doing the right thing, for Joseph's sake,' said Elizabeth Relph.

'You'll lead a very civilized, comfortable life here. He's a very fortunate man. He has said so, himself.'

'He knows so little about me. Sometimes I feel I know so little myself.'

She went to stand in the doorway, staring out with her cheek against the stone jamb. Her dress bunched on one enticing hip and fell away down the contour of her leg.

'I shall have to get used to his routine, and whatever the precedents and precedences are in his way of life.'

'That shouldn't be too alarming. You must have learnt the form in India.'

Her laugh was not a happy one. 'Oh, yes, I had many a lesson there. Whom one invites to tiffin, and whom one doesn't. Where a mere Assistant Collector's wife stands during a Governor's visit, and where she sits at the Residency table — if she's allowed to get that far.'

'I think Mr. Hinde will prove less rigorous.'

'I shall not mind too much what he expects, if . . . '

She was communing with herself rather than with him. 'There was one pattern for life on the plains,' she murmured. 'And within it, one pattern for the administrators and one for the military. And in the hot months, one thing for the men still at work and another for the wives sent up to the hill stations. That was what turned me to the study of the eastern religions. I wanted to find the true soul of that land, not the one we had imported. But I was told I mustn't demean myself in that way, it was setting a bad example: I ran the risk of taking it seriously. But when it was all over and I was back in this country. Back home . . . ' She tried the word and found it wanting.

Now she was as still and meditative as the statue.

Caspian murmured: 'That was when you were drawn into the circle of the veiled woman?'

'Veiled woman? No, I don't remember. I know I wandered down some strange byways in search of . . . of sustenance. Because of what I had experienced in India, I met Madame Blavatsky and hoped for an answer in the Theosophical Society. But there was no inner peace there: only feuds and squabbles. And the

Hermetic Society — no, that was too western and beyond my grasp. Yet I wanted just a little comfort.' She pushed herself away from the doorway. 'And still . . . all these years . . . I've been troubled by the notion of another self, wanting to be freed. Another me, wanting to be herself.' She began to move out into the sunlight, casting back at Caspian a wry glance, sensing he was one of the rare men who might understand this. 'If she does break loose,' she said, 'I pray she'll do Joseph no lasting harm.'

Beyond her, Bronwen and Thornhill came into view, walking side by side towards the temple.

Elizabeth and Caspian went down the two steps from the plinth to meet them.

Bronwen raised a faintly querulous eyebrow at her husband. It was useless to try suppressing the sensations Elizabeth had awoken in him. He briefly let Bronwen share them, and felt her appreciative physical response; and was teased by her mock reproof.

But it's you I love.

She purred a silent answer.

'Well, Caspian. Seems to have sorted itself out, hey?' Thornhill was in a bluffly magnanimous mood. 'Storm in a test tube. With a happy reaction in the end.'

Across the lawn sang the note of the dinner gong. The four of them began to stroll towards the house. A few yards from the terrace steps Thornhill came to a halt.

'Good God, would you believe it!' He took out his watch, flipped open the cover, and shook his head. 'D'you know, I have the most urgent appointment, and here I am . . . '

He looked about him, in familiar territory suddenly and inexplicably lost.

Caspian and Bronwen felt the throb of a summons higher and more ethereal than the second call of the dinner gong: a shimmer of sound at the limit of hearing, like the vibration of a glass accidentally struck by a fork.

'You're not thinking of running away now?' Elizabeth tried to take Thornhill's arm.

He drew away. 'D'you think you could make my excuses to Joseph? Really must be off.'

Thornhill veered towards the drive with the apparent intention of striding down it and out into the road, where one supposed he would seek a cab. His steps were those of an automaton.

Caspian sprang forward and caught his arm.

'Sir Andrew, you can't go.'

The mesmeric command throbbed more insistently.

It will be tonight. You are ready, all is ready.

It took all Caspian's force to bring Thornhill at last to a standstill.

'My dear Doctor, this is most unseemly. I'll ask you to release me.' It was his ordinary tone, yet sly and unsteady. He was impatient to be gone.

Of your own free will. You will not turn back?

'No,' said Thornhill. He began to struggle again. 'Caspian, I'll not endure this.'

'If you have any explaining to do,' said Caspian, 'you must do it to our host in person.'

'What explanations are called for?'

Hinde was waiting in the open doorway for them to come through and join him.

Thornhill wrested his arm away from Caspian and began to babble. Excuses spilled out of him, tumbling over one another, and he laughed at Hinde's puzzled frown. 'I'm mad, Joseph, you must know that by now. Gone clean out of my head, the most important meeting — can't let a whole roomful of them down, can I? I know you'll never forgive me. But at least I offer my sincere congratulations. Lucky fellow. Lucky fellow.' He swung towards Elizabeth, seized her hand, and kissed it. 'You'll have a quieter evening without me.'

Hinde, with a dignity quite remote from his frequent stuffiness, said: 'Andrew, I should take the gravest exception to your leaving now.'

'Sorry, my duty is to my first appointment. Damn fool, all right, I know, to get in such a muddle.'

Caspian and Bronwen stood behind him, so that when he turned to go he would have to go between them, or round them.

If he left, could they follow him, and be led to the priestess?

But it would be inexcusable for other guests to follow suit.

Now Thornhill spun round; and faced the Caspians.

They heard the command swoop up the octave to an intolerable shriek. Abruptly it whined away again, growing fainter as it sped towards the far edge of the world.

Thornhill gave a little moan of deprivation.

Caspian slid his arm through his wife's. They caught a faint whisper rustling through Thornhill's head from that ever-increasing distance.

Stay. It will be achieved.

'You promised.' Thornhill said it aloud, to empty air.

We shall assemble where you are. Stay.

'Our other guests are waiting,' said Hinde glacially.

Still in a daze, Thornhill turned away from Caspian and Bronwen, and escorted Elizabeth up the steps.

At the dining table he was unusually

subdued for some considerable time, reaching for solace from his glass. It was emptied and refilled with increasing frequency. Bronwen was his neighbour on one side, Mrs. Dampier on the other. Mrs. Dampier, the naturally high colour of her cheeks intensified by wine and excitement, bobbed forward to make fluttery jokes about her host's new responsibilities and how he would have to mend his ways. Slowly Bronwen engaged Thornhill in conversation. At first he kept his head bowed sullenly over his glass and replied in monosyllables. Then, animated like Mrs. Dampier by the wine, he managed a smile, a protest, a burst of refutation. Caspian was talking to Laura and could catch only the general rise and fall of other conversation. It was not until he relinquished Laura to the awkwardly attentive Robert Dampier on her other side that he could eavesdrop, while appearing to devote all his attention to his food.

'Don't know what came over me,' Thornhill was saying. 'One minute I couldn't imagine what I was doing here, and the next I couldn't imagine what I'd be doing anywhere else. Strain of overwork . . . '

Bronwen's voice sank to an undertone and she was conscious of Caspian speaking through her: 'You're in very real danger.'

Thornhill drank and spluttered with laughter.

'Danger? Nonsense, m'dear. Just because I had a bit of a turn out there?'

On Caspian's right, Elizabeth Relph said: 'Dr. Caspian, do you suppose your wife would agree to come to the house in a week or two to take some pictures of Joseph and myself? Perhaps we can settle a time before you leave this evening.'

Laura Hinde was animatedly talking to young Dampier. Completely in control of herself, she smiled, charmingly covered the gaps in Robert's stammering conversation, and was obviously practising with growing assurance the arts which would one day, with the right man, be deployed to devastating effect. Robert Dampier was not the man; but there would be one, when she was ready.

Voices clashed sociably. Hinde's gaze strayed to Elizabeth's smooth white throat and the rise of her breasts, and once her gaze slowly engaged his and they smiled and turned to carry on conversations elsewhere.

Thornhill chased a mutton cutlet through a heap of peas with his fork. He hiccupped. His slurred voice rose.

'Quite wrong, my dear Mrs. Caspian. Necromancy? Not at all, not at all. We discarded all those notions of raising dead substances and tinkering with charms or potions generations ago. But the psychological aspects of natural science — ah, now, that's a different matter.' He chewed for a while, washed a troublesome morsel down with a gulp of hock. 'Our ancestors, now, not much more than a hundred and fifty years ago, saw blankets giving off sparks in cold weather. And strange lights in the night, and God's lightning and thunderbolts. Supernatural? Today we know all about harnessing electricity. It has no more mysteries for us. And there are other forces we shall soon learn to control. Things well worth investigating. Not sneering at them and not being scared of them simply because of our own ignorance. Experiment. Investigate. The only way we've progressed from scrabbling about in caves.'

Caspian wondered whether, in the middle of Thornhill's befuddled bombast, there might yet come another summons this evening, more imperative or more subtle; silencing him in mid-sentence and luring him to some hidden rendezvous.

★   ★   ★

Slowly Wentworth took off his hat and climbed back up the stairs. Annie had her legs tucked under her on the sofa and was looking remotely into the fire. She raised her head and peered at him from under a tendril of hair.

'Forgotten something?'

In fact he had forgotten where he had been intending to go, but knew it was no longer important. Something had somehow been cancelled out. He took his coat off and draped it idly across the back of a chair.

Annie tried again. 'Thought you was off this minute.'

'Yes, so did I.'

He held out his hands to the fire, as puzzled as she was. Some compulsion had seized him but now had slackened its grip.

'To the warehouse, you said,' she reminded him.

The warehouse: yes, that was it, of course. But it was no longer urgent. 'It can wait.'

'Dotty time of night to go there anyway.' Annie studied his face slyly. 'So what'll we do?'

'Something special?' he said.

She picked herself up from the sofa, uncurling and stretching like a cat, tautening from a fireside animal to a predator.

Beyond her he saw a stack of recent periodicals on the occasional table. One booklet that stuck out caught his attention. He did not recognize it, though it must have been something he had bought: Annie was not in the habit of visiting booksellers or newsvendors.

At his shoulder someone was telling him he must go and pick it up.

'Now what's the matter?'

It was Annie speaking. But Annie was in front of the fire, not at his shoulder.

She.

He walked past Annie and pulled the wad of pages out of the pile. They fell open of their own accord and he read the first paragraph.

His heart thumped. What had made him pick the thing up? Why hadn't he noticed it before now? He returned to the monstrous, scurrilous words and finished the section. Then he smacked the crumpled paper against his palm. 'Look at this! Look at it!'

The typography of Hansard's *Parliamentary Debates* allowed no scope for enticing illustrations, and the text itself did not offer the kind of provocation Wentworth relished.

'I'll have to go out for an hour or two.'

'But you only just this minute said we was going to — '

'I can't let this rest. It's outrageous. Attacking me — me! — in the House of Commons. What do you make of that?'

'In the House of Commons?' Annie sniggered. 'What yer been up to, then?'

'With no chance to defend myself. Turning the country against me, as if scholars like myself weren't providing an essential part of the country's needs.' He tore the pages open again. 'Listen to this: 'In a courtyard not far from the Strand, masquerading as a bookshop for supplying the wants of serious students of philosophy and anthropology (for anthropology is the fashionable euphemism nowadays), there operates a complete factory supplying the most depraved wants. A factory devoted to the literature of wickedness, a literature which has played no small part in spreading disease and peopling our prisons and reformatories with lechers and scapegraces. When will these iniquities be stamped out? Are men such as the proprietor of that loathsome den in the heart of London to be allowed to spread their plague, like something carried by the swiftest and foulest of rats throughout our land?' Wentworth wiped a fleck of spittle from his lips. 'I'll have him outside the House of Commons, where he'll not be so well protected. At his own home. Yes, what about that? Oh, yes, we'll see whether he's so brave with his slanders then.'

'It can wait till morning.'

'It can *not* wait till morning.'

'Oh, why did you have to pick that thing up tonight?' she said peevishly.

He reached for his coat. She was in his way. He raised his fist to knock her aside. There were things to be done this evening, things she was too stupid to understand. Ducking under his arm she tried to wriggle against him. His appetite for her was quite gone.

'You're in my way!' he shouted.

Why was she staring at him like that, as if he were a stranger — or as if she were somebody else, goading him, leering at him?

He turned away. His old coat wasn't good enough. He took his best ulster with its smart, short cape from the hook at the top of the stairs. Since he was to have a dispute with a Member of Parliament it should be done in style.

Annie followed him to the door. 'Aren't you goin' to kiss me, anyway?'

He shouldered past her. *Time to be rid of her.*

Only when he was out in the evening air, striding across the court, did horror overtake him. What misleading devil had turned him so savagely against his dear little Annie, an unnatural desire to be done with everything he had known, and move on?

To where?

His footsteps slowed. He wanted to turn back and throw himself at Annie's feet, demanding that she punish him for his treachery.

But he was driven on as if someone behind were whipping him into a trot.

Everything would be all right. There must be a reason behind it, all part of the wonderful plan.

During the drive to Chiswick he forced his mind to concentrate on what lay ahead, rehearsing his attack. Hinde thought himself no end of a debater. This time he'd meet his match. Undoubtedly a servant answering the door would try to come between them. But while that servant was consulting his master, Wentworth would storm unceremoniously in and make it clear that he would not be easily ejected.

Hinde must be made to listen.

He dismissed the hansom before realizing the full length of the entrance drive. Trudging through the dusk he saw that the front door was open, flooding the portico with light. A carriage stood there; a number of people were chatting and shaking hands.

Stay. We shall assemble where you are.

Heads turned towards him, but the voice was not one of theirs.

Wentworth had not foreseen an audience. Perhaps it could be used to his advantage. He would shame Hinde before his own friends. And if violence were offered, he would expose them all in court, under oath. Then they would have to speak the truth.

He reached the portico and, squaring his shoulders, strode into the light.

His quarry was easy enough to identify. The peremptory manner was just what one might have expected.

'Who are you, sir?'

'Well may you ask.'

Hinde came between his guests and faced Wentworth. 'This is an unusual hour of the evening to be making an unannounced call.'

'The circumstances are in every way unusual not to say unsavoury.'

'Sedgwick.' Hinde glanced back over his shoulder. 'Perhaps you'll come and ask this gentleman for his card and the nature of his business.'

'No need for any intermediary,' said Wentworth. 'I've come here to speak to you face to face — this instant.'

'You're insolent, sir.'

'To match your own insolence. Standing up in Parliament and denigrating those of whom you know nothing — those who work for the pleasure of thousands, but happen to displease petty puritans like you.'

'Get off my property immediately.'

'Scared that your fine friends may hear what a coward you are?'

Hinde raised a fist. One of his guests, a tall swaggering fellow with a dark beard, stepped to his side.

'Two of you?' jeered Wentworth. 'And two or three more if needed, doubtless. Suppressing truth by any means within your power: censorship, slander, and brute force. That's the policy of your Government, isn't it?'

Hinde's arm sank to his side. 'State your business and let's be done with you. But no man slanders me with — '

'Slander? You can let such a word pass your lips?' From under his cape Wentworth drew the folded *Hansard* and brandished it before Hinde's nose. 'Is this not a cowardly slander? Shielding behind Parliamentary privilege while abusing the good name of one who strives to provide the decent, healthy public with what it requires.'

'Ah,' said Hinde. 'I see. Would I be right in supposing you to be the proprietor of that noisome gutter of a bookshop in Kemble Court?'

'You wouldn't dare publish your abuse outside the House of Commons, where I could exercise my rights against you in the courts.'

'I will dare whenever it suits me. I shall publish, have no fear, and you shall be damned.' Hinde took a step forward. Wentworth held his ground. 'And now I'll thank you to leave these premises. Make an appointment with me and we'll thrash this matter out at a more suitable time.'

'We can thrash it out now. I haven't come all this way just to be — '

'Leave, sir, before I take measures to make you leave.'

As Hinde nodded, a younger man in coachman's livery came past him and took Wentworth's arm in a painful grip.

'You'll have me assaulted?' raged Wentworth.

'I'll exercise every Englishman's right,' said Hinde, 'to have a violent and unwelcome visitor escorted off his premises.'

The young man twisted Wentworth round to face the drive. When he tried to resist, his forearm was brought up so excruciatingly that he stooped, gasped, and stumbled a few steps away from the door and into the night.

'You may walk through those gates at your own pace,' said Hinde, 'or you may be accompanied there by Atkinson.'

'When you have the courage to listen — '

'When you have the courtesy to make a proper appointment, I shall be prepared

to listen to your case. If you have one.'
Hinde snapped his fingers. 'All right,
Atkinson. Release him.'

'Very good, sir.'

The iron grip slackened. Wentworth
wanted to rub his arm but would not do
so before those gloating eyes. Damn every
one of them.

He shouted: 'You've not heard the last
of this!'

The man was waiting to seize him
again at the slightest provocation. Swal-
lowing his pride and fury, Wentworth
walked with a slow, deliberate tread along
the drive.

He was some yards from the gates
when there was a clatter of hoofs and
wheels on the gravel behind him. He
threw himself into the shadows of a small
plantation, and a departing coach rushed
past him. Its passengers would no doubt
have regarded it as a great joke if he had
been run down. He leaned against a tree,
regaining his breath. No, Joseph Hinde
had assuredly not heard the last of this!

★　★　★

'The impertinence of it,' said Hinde. 'For such a thing to happen, on this evening of all evenings.'

The Dampiers had driven away. The remaining guests went back indoors, but Bronwen nodded to Caspian that she thought it time for them, too, to make their goodbyes.

'You must take a glass of port with me.' Hinde held open the door of the library for Bronwen to go through. 'To take away the taste of that deplorable incident.'

'You suffer from many disgruntled electors beating a path to your door?' asked Caspian sympathetically.

'It's rare for one to come to the house itself, and in such intemperate mood.' Hinde looked round. 'Where's Andrew? I thought the mention of a glass of port would have brought him in without more ado.'

Caspian looked back into the hall.

Some fleeting intimation jerked his head up to follow the curve of the staircase.

There was nobody on it, and nobody at the top. Yet he had a sensation of someone running heavily but silently; someone there a moment ago and now out of sight.

Bronwen had been resting her fingers on a large library globe. When she snatched her hand away, the sphere began to spin wildly.

Together she and Caspian were running.

He led the way, racing up two treads at a time. On the first landing he hesitated only a second. Higher yet. They both knew it, felt it, heard the summons.

And felt Thornhill's answering, drunken ecstasy.

Spirit of air and etheric force. The flight and the fulfilment . . . answering yow laws . . . through eternity, eternity . . .

In darkness they blundered along a narrow corridor. There was faint, muted light at the end: the light of the sky and distant houses, seen through an open casement.

They reached the opening on to the balcony.

Thornhill was balancing in solemn drunken absorption on the balcony rail. His head was magnificent against the night sky. The world lay winking and sparkling beyond and below him. He was a comic figure; and a frightening one.

Caspian stood quite still. Coming up behind him, Bronwen steadied herself against his shoulder.

Don't look down, Caspian pleaded silently. *Don't look down, or you'll fall.*

But what if it was his whole intention to fall?

They felt the world tilting before Thornhill. He was being invited to look down. Ordered to look down. Inexorably his gaze was controlled, lowered.

You will not turn back?

They did not dare to cry out or move another inch.

Thornhill reached the end of the rail. He must now, Caspian estimated, be above the end of the terrace. And he was looking down at what lay below. As if through those tranced eyes, Caspian saw the dark upthrust of the jagged ornamental urn, waiting to impale him.

Thornhill tensed.

To one side, below, someone opened a door, and a lop-sided triangle of light was etched on the mossy stones. A shadow scuttled below the rim of the terrace; another, distorted by the glow of the lamps, seemed to grope and swim out from the house. Arms of shadow clutched and dissolved.

Thornhill looked out joyfully across the world and spread his arms wide.

They could not reach him with their hands. But into his mind Caspian and Bronwen struck with all the power they possessed — not attacking but encircling, trying to curl round and enclose his thoughts, tug them gently back to reality.

This way . . . along here . . . slowly . . .

Fury was unleashed against their intrusion. A savage riposte stabbed into their own minds. They reeled as Thornhill reeled, but held on to him.

In his head there was a strident command.

You will not turn back.

Battered and jostled from side to side, he staggered a few steps back along the rail. *This way.* He tottered. His head lolled round until he was no longer staring out into the beckoning night. With infinite slowness he began to fall: to topple and fall inwards, coming down on his left shoulder and crumpling at Caspian's feet. For a moment he was shocked into numbness. Then, head still lolling, he heaved himself up so that his chin was on his knees. He began to whimper; retched; and despairingly, uncontrollably vomited over his knees and legs and feet.

On the terrace below, Elizabeth Relph stepped into the light and looked up at the deserted balustrade.

10

In such a condition the fellow was obviously incapable of making his own way home tonight. Hinde looked on in disgust as his valet sponged Thornhill down and then helped him gingerly to his feet. Once divested of those reeking clothes he would have to be provided with others, and with a bed for the night.

'I'm obliged to you,' he said brusquely to Caspian. 'If he'd gone the other way, even that thick skull would hardly have survived intact.'

The evening had been ruined. First that insufferable creature thrusting himself into their midst, and now this drunken cavorting — and this nauseating mess and stench.

He ought never to have invited Andrew Thornhill; or, having invited him, ought to have kept closer watch on the amount of drink he was putting away inside him.

Dr. Caspian said: 'He was in great peril

this evening. My wife tried to warn him.'

'When Andrew's in his cups he'll heed no warnings.'

'There was more to it than the wine.'

Thornhill mumbled what might have been an attempt at an apology, but turned into a pitiful howl. He stared past Hinde at Caspian. 'Why did you drag me back? You . . . d'you know what you've done?'

'Andrew,' said Hinde sharply, 'if Dr. Caspian hadn't been there to save you from your own folly — '

'Save me? She was here. Here, I tell you. I felt her, I was going, we knew what we were doing. We knew. Is she still here? If there's time, if she's still here . . . '

Elizabeth reached the top of the stairs and stood to one side as the valet helped Thornhill to lurch past.

She said: 'I didn't know what to do. I could see him from where I was, but I didn't dare move or call out in case I distracted him.'

Hinde put his arm round her.

'Why was I stopped?' Thornhill's wail died away.

Hinde said: 'Put him in the Wyatt room.'

'Very good, sir.'

When the stairs were clear, Hinde indicated that Dr. and Mrs. Caspian should precede Elizabeth and himself down to the hall and the open door of the library.

'I hope he'll be safe,' said Caspian dubiously.

'I'm putting him in the old nursery. With bars across the window.'

'The night's not over. The conjunctions — '

'He'll sleep it off, never fear.'

Elizabeth touched his hand. Their fingers moved shyly together and then were stroked apart again.

'It's time I left. Unless you need some help.'

'With Andrew? Not a task for you, my dear.'

Caspian said: 'We'll gladly drive Mrs. Relph home.'

'It's out of your way, Doctor,' Hinde said, 'and I've already arranged for my coachman to make the journey.'

He wished the evening to be concluded, as a botched Bill in Parliament might be abandoned and written off.

Caspian and his wife seemed ill at ease.

'Seriously, Mr. Hinde, I trust you'll keep a careful watch on Sir Andrew. At least until morning.'

'Seriously, Doctor, I'll keep the most careful watch. On him and on my wine cellar.'

★ ★ ★

The hooded gig turned out of the gates and rolled slowly eastwards. At this late hour Caspian would normally have set a fast pace for the light vehicle. Tonight Bronwen could tell that every inch added between them and Nasmyth Lodge was acting like a brake-shoe on the wheels.

She tried to comfort him. 'We could scarcely have invited ourselves to stay the night.'

'Or to have forced ourselves on Mrs. Relph.'

'Quite so.'

'But we ought to be in one place or the other. For it's not ended yet, I'll swear it.'

He let the horse slacken to no more than a saunter.

Bronwen said: 'Who's in the greater danger?'

'Thornhill, without a doubt. I don't know that Mrs. Relph is in any danger at all.'

'But you think she poses a threat?'

They clip-clopped along, the reins slack in Caspian's hand. He said: 'Tonight was Thornhill's night to die. Voluntarily, like the other two. In the previous cases the hair and nail snippets were collected as an essential part of the ritual. They must have been equally necessary on this occasion. So the woman, the priestess, the veiled one ... she ... must have been there waiting.'

Waiting out of sight for Thornhill to fall to his death. No, not to fall: to dive willingly. And she had had to be close enough to snatch what she needed and make off with it. They remembered the siren shadows tempting Thornhill to the brink; and the shadow of Elizabeth Relph, and then Elizabeth herself stepping out on to the terrace.

Bronwen shifted in her seat. 'No, I can't associate Elizabeth with ritual murder.

Whatever she suffered in the past, her repudiation of it all was genuine.'

'In one mood, yes.'

'But now there is only one mood for her. Happiness. She was so happy with Hinde, with their engagement, with everything.'

'Except her other self. She spoke to me about another part of her which has not yet been allowed to emerge.'

An ominous cloud thickened in Bronwen's mind. Still she shook her head. She would not, could not be so wrong about Elizabeth.

'She tried to make a joke of it,' said Caspian, 'but supposing she has good reason to worry about that other personality — about being possessed by it?'

The gig came to a stop in the deserted street.

Bronwen protested: 'Early this evening Thornhill was summoned to meet that veiled woman. But at that time Elizabeth was at Nasmyth Lodge, no more than a few yards away from him. She couldn't have been somewhere else, sending messages for him to dash off and meet her.'

'If there were another personality hidden within her, though, or hidden in anyone else . . . '

Anyone else. Not Laura still in danger, when she had seemed so free and happy? Was she still unknowingly a doomed victim, the fire element being saved for some long-calculated end — or something worse, something scheming and active and insidious?

'Any hidden entity within either of those young women,' Bronwen agreed reluctantly, 'might lie dormant until the appointed time.'

'Until that alarm clock we spoke of sounds its signal. And when the signal sounded for Thornhill — '

'She'd realize after his first instinctive response that circumstances had changed. When decreeing the original appointment she couldn't have foreseen that when the time actually came round they would be together under the same roof.' The hood of the gig seemed to be closing in and stifling her. 'You think we should follow Elizabeth and keep watch?'

'That would leave Thornhill unguarded.

He's the one in the greatest danger until this night's over.'

He turned the horse and gig and now set a faster trot. Astral influences prevailing over Thornhill's birth might not move entirely out of their significant aspects for several hours. The woman would be desperate to complete this stage of the cycle tonight while those influences remained powerful, and might come again for him.

'We can hardly present ourselves on the doorstep,' said Bronwen, 'demanding shelter for the night.'

A lane skirted the railings down the western edge of the estate, past the little temple. It widened to make a turning-place near a side gate and a gardener's shed, narrowed again, and petered out under the Thames towpath. Caspian drove cautiously to the end.

A line of poplars shielded the end of the lane from the riverbank. Between them and the dense shrubbery within the railings was a secluded corner of darkness, which no casual eye would penetrate. A casual passer-by was in any case unlikely at this hour of the night. Caspian led the horse from the shafts and tethered it loosely to one of the trees. He propped the shafts level between the railings, so that he and Bronwen could sit back comfortably under the hood, and took a rug from the locker beneath the seat.

They settled themselves with hands touching above the rug, eyes closed, letting muscle and mind go slack.

Against a background ebb and flow of dreams from the fringes of the city came the steadier pulse of the house: drowsy, with an occasional fidget of resentment which might have been Hinde's vexation at the way his evening had turned out.

'It feels as if they're all still there.' Bronwen was not picking out individual strands of consciousness: it was simply a feeling of wholeness, of the circle unbroken — unbroken but slowly and remorselessly contracting. 'You think Elizabeth turned and came straight back, as quickly as we did?'

'Whoever the woman is, she's very determined. And very powerful.'

His hand on hers counselled patience. Sleep and dream thickened about

259

them. They let themselves drift on a viscous tide of unknowing, their minds lazily open like the petal tentacles of a sea anemone waiting for what might stray into their embrace.

The time is coming again. I shall be born again.

It was a whisper but a clear, greedy one. They waited. It would be fatal to snatch at it, perhaps frighten it away. Let it repeat itself, or continue, drifting closer, not knowing they were listening and interpreting.

They glimpsed a veiled woman leaning forward in a chair. She was hunched and meditative, slowly awakening to knowledge she had forgotten. She might have been drowsing a lifetime in that chair; or for no longer than Bronwen and Caspian had been sunk in their reverie; and now was reassembling her memories and from them gaining strength to move on to the next stage.

Fire and water, earth and air, renew me.

The picture was more vivid than any photograph Bronwen could ever have hoped to take. And now it moved: moved as a dream does, condensing days and centuries and places.

It steadied in what they somehow knew to be the year 1534.

I am the wife. I am queen.

She was queen. But so were fifteen others — consorts of the self-proclaimed Anabaptist king, the anarchic John of Leyden. Also there were his concubines, tempting and flattering him until he wearied of them and discarded them. Out of the gloating mind of this woman spreading like a greasy wrack over the Caspians' minds, came a procession of women through the Münster market-place on their way to vilification, humiliation and execution. Once rid of them, King John would turn back to one of his wives for comfort, to another for amusement; and to a freshly recruited concubine for sudden lust though he knew that boredom must follow. Boredom for him, denunciation and death for her.

I am Queen Theodora. They were rich times: fearful times but rich ones, for those who did not flinch.

I made him burn for me ten times

more than for the others. I refused him,
tormented him, made him pay.

Hated him.

Insisted on the death of Elizabeth,
whom I loved.

Words blurred and became writhing images.
In timeless rooms with impalpable walls
two women clung together, fought apart,
laughed and rejoined each other in an
ecstasy that their lord and master had
never provoked in their bodies.

Until Elizabeth betrayed Theodora with
another of the wives — because of the
disgust that had replaced passion — disgust at the stains and blotches of the foul
pox on Theodora's arms and body. King
John had visited this on her. Elizabeth
spurned her. They must both be destroyed.

She began, now, to remember. Had she
not lived before? Would she not go on
living, in whatever form she chose, if she
honoured the ritual? To escape from this
disease-ridden frame into a younger,
sweeter one — there had been something
of that in her love for Elizabeth, but now
it should be made real and lasting.

John would grant her wishes. There

were two of his concubines she craved as her personal handmaidens, having carefully verified their birth dates. Also, under another sign of the zodiac, there was a man whom John had been torturing and for whose torn body she pleaded. The wretch was grateful to accept from her a voluntary, swifter death. And there was Elizabeth, born under the sign of fire. Elizabeth too must will her own death.

It was not difficult to arrange for John to come upon this fair queen of his with a younger woman. When he reviled her she cursed him back with all the hatred that had built up within her. She screamed her revulsion at his foul body and foul soul, his lechery and his bestial laws, and demanded to be set free from this hypocritical court of his.

When he had racked and beaten her until she begged for death, John whipped her out into the market square. Theodora led the procession of his other wives, and the townsfolk were driven into the square to witness the king's justice. Queen Elizabeth declared proudly that she welcomed death; and he smote off her head. Now it was a dance that Theodora led, chanting 'Gloria in Excelsis' as the women made a squealing, jostling ring about the blood-soaked corpse. At the end of the day the remains were flung upon a fire, and the smoke drifted for hours down the narrow side streets and under the lowering eaves.

Yet somehow the dance went on — went on forever. Faces reeled faster and faster, running together into a blur of masks with open mouths and a thousand eyes. A thousand dreams spun in the whirlpool of limbo.

I am Theodora; I was Theodora; I am free, I am new, I am immortal.

One face steadied among the others. It was the face of Laura, of a potential Laura, a Laura as yet unborn. Then it was sucked down into the heart of the maelstrom.

I am free.

She was there among the crowd, daughter of a secretly Catholic family at last daring to declare itself as the Hessian troops approached and the rule of the Anabaptists drew to its close. She was there with the townsfolk praying for the soul of John of Leyden while rejoicing at his fate when, in that same market-place where Elizabeth had died to release Theodora, he was torn to death with red-hot pincers and the scorched, dripping fragments hauled up in a basket to the pinnacle of the church tower.

Faces eddied again, went on eddying and forming and dissolving and reforming over the decades and centuries.

I am Nell, I shall never die.

Evelina, treading the boards disguised as a boy, tasting dangerous delights and learning, choosing opportunities, knowing when the elements must combine again and when it was time to be gone . . .

Time to change.

I am Elizabeth Báthory, Countess Nadasdy.

Her husband, richest and most honoured of Habsburg commanders in the Carpathians, was often away. When she was with child by a virile manservant she went to stay with an aunt.

And was delivered of Ilona.

I name you Ilona. You shall learn from me and take over what I have carried within me all these centuries, all I have tasted and heard and experienced.

Ilona was placed in a good home, secluded, waiting.

The young Countess Elizabeth pursued her pleasures, most lovingly and devoutly the pleasures of pain: other people's pain. She conjured up those older delights from the days in Münster and, with renewed vigour, whipped her slaves more assiduously on. In the first weeks of marriage she had passed some idle hours disfiguring a maidservant presented to her by her husband. Now she studied many more refinements.

Occasionally Ilona paid an unobtrusive visit and was allowed to sit silently watching; and learning.

Scores of the girls hired to work in the castle came to know the moment when the Countess, on a sudden pretext that their sewing was shoddy or their behaviour insolent, would take them to the sunken room murmured of as Her Ladyship's Punishment Chamber. Those who knew of it only by repute dreaded the hour when they would know too much.

Few ever went back to their peasant

homesteads. But parents did not dare to protest. Nobody dared even refuse to supply another daughter for the Countess's service.

And then came the great revelation. The joy of it seethed as strongly in her mind after nigh on three centuries. Bronwen could not bear to listen, and to see; but could not bear to draw away and break the link.

As blood from dying girls splashed over Elizabeth Báthory's bare shoulders and arms, she saw her skin becoming softer and milkier. After weeks of floggings and stabbings she was younger than ever. Her husband commented on it when he came home; rhapsodized sadly over her, when he had to leave. She had discovered the ultimate secret of immortality. She would never wither, she would remain beautiful for eternity, if only she bathed in blood every day.

They were brought in from all over her husband's lands, the country girls whose lifeblood was to preserve her. Four hundred of them, five hundred . . . questions were asked and then silenced . . . six hundred . . .

Beautiful forever.

Her husband was dead. But in eternity there would be other men, other joys, and always the joy of bloodletting and smoothing fresh life into her skin.

She set up another important room in the vast castle, which was now all hers, peopled mainly by women but with a few trustworthy men to satisfy her spasmodic needs. This time the chamber was for the practice of black magic. Blood and magic became one.

Forever.

Until the princes and her own relatives came to condemn her and to see for themselves the room of blood and the room of blackness, the bones buried away, the disfigured corpses and the collection of secret grimoires. To condemn those servants who had ministered to her appetites and then burn their bodies alive, but by reason of family pressure to spare Elizabeth's life and sentence her to lifelong imprisonment in the haunted cellars of her castle.

Lifelong? But she was immortal, she could not spend eternity in a dungeon.

They did not understand. Somebody must be made to understand.

Few favours were granted her. But when she was nigh to death and begged forgiveness, at her most earnest request they allowed her daughter Ilona to be sent to her. Ilona brought in her company two young girls, who were forthwith abducted by the castle guards: at least, that was the most plausible story to explain the disappearance of all four of them. It was, after all, unthinkable that the dying and repentant Countess should have the strength to play at her appalling magic again, even though there was also a rumour about a little scullery maid whose corpse was found half-drained of blood in one of the castle drains. Unthinkable and unverifiable, since Elizabeth Báthory died so soon after the final meeting with her daughter: 'without a crucifix,' said the report on her last hours, 'and without light.'

I am Ilona.

Ilona left the castle with bowed head and a secret smile, which few were allowed to see. She continued to be well-spoken of for her piety and gentleness, and many acquaintances were touched by the particular note which came into her voice when she spoke of her late mother. Yet often there was a gleam in her eye, which discomfited those who came too close; and the servants who had once loved her now went warily.

The Caspians' minds were flooded by a torrent of pictures which Ilona had accumulated during those visits to her mother and which she now longed to recreate in flesh and blood. Mother and daughter were one, and one with untold predecessors devoted to those primordial rites and pleasures, which must never be allowed to die.

I was before Ilona, and was Ilona and am Ilona, and shall be named as I choose and nameless when I choose, born and reborn, again and yet again . . .

The veiled woman crouched forward into the painful dazzle of their vision clawing out to retrieve something which had slipped through her fingers. They felt her physical nearness. Not in the house; closer than that, preparing to spring.

The ache of sustaining awareness of her without betraying themselves grew more acute.

The chair. Through Caspian's memory they saw it simultaneously the chair in that little temple, to which she had come secretly and where she now sat facing the half-open door.

She stood up. She was moving swiftly towards the door

Come now. The summons to Thornhill sang, high above hearing across the lawn.

Caspian leaned involuntarily forward and aped her movement as he made to spring from the gig.

In a flash she was aware of them. The full power of her mind raked round like the beam of a lighthouse into Bronwen's head. *You again! Who are you?* White fire was a blinding, scorching circlet of agony. There came a thrust of bitter laughter such as she had once heard in the tumult of Laura's mind.

So. Now I know you. And shall know you again.

The discord of merriment raged up as Caspian came to Bronwen's rescue, pouring strength and healing into their mental barriers so that the murderous light was dimmed and then sealed off altogether.

A dark figure burst from the temple colonnade and ran across the grass.

Caspian set one foot on a shaft of the gig and got a grip on the top of the railings. He swung his knees up between his arms with acrobatic confidence, setting his feet between the spikes. Then he was over into the shrubbery beyond and crashing through to the lawn.

A sleepwalking shadow came out on the terrace. Even in such uncertain light the figure was unmistakably Thornhill's.

From where Bronwen stood, the woman appeared to be setting an incredible pace. But Caspian was heading her off. She would not reach her prey on the terrace before their paths crossed.

Bronwen sensed that his first move when he was upon the woman would be to tear the veil from her face. What would they see: what fury would be unleashed?

Desperately the shadow doubled back towards the gates.

'Where are you?' pleaded Thornhill, entranced in despair.

Bronwen felt the fever abating and the predatory mind escaping, convulsed by a poisonous rage. One mind: or two?

Caspian's steps slackened. He could not catch the creature now. As the figure dwindled, so the circle that had tightened in their minds slackened and split. The sense of wholeness was shattered. And still Bronwen was gripped by her conviction that the ritual was being abandoned not just by the running woman but by another: of not just one but two of them making their escape.

Thornhill, giving up? But Thornhill was not trying to run. He stood, sagging pitifully, on the terrace.

'Who's that out there?' Hope was draining from his voice. 'Who are you . . . where . . . ?'

The two had gone.

Caspian abandoned the chase and turned away, loping back to the railings and back over them, to harness the horse and turn the gig back up the lane.

Light was touching chimneys and

rooftops. The whiteness of the Nasmyth Lodge balcony began to gleam.

Thornhill, unappreciative of the fact, was safe. It was dawn.

11

He let himself into the shop and locked the door again behind him. Making a space on the counter, he opened the case of books he had carried in, and studied the titles. He was a mite puzzled by one or two of them. He had taken one light case to the warehouse and brought this heavier one back, and now wondered why he had chosen these particular volumes. Or why he had gone there in the first place, at this time of the morning.

There were too many incidents like this nowadays. He was forgetting too many things.

Somewhere, somehow, there had been a promise that he would get better soon. Things were becoming absurd and not a little perturbing when he could not account for his movements over a mere matter of hours.

He went upstairs. Annie, tousled with sleep, was waiting at the top.

'And where d'you think you've been? Out all night, coming in for your breakfast like some old tomcat . . . You've been off with a woman somewhere!'

'No. I've been . . . walking.'

'All night? I'm not good enough for you any more, I s'pose.'

She pranced away into the sitting room. He followed. She was wearing only the long pink shift with a scalloped hem in which she went to bed and in which she often slouched about for half the day.

The sun had still not risen high enough to strike down into the courtyard. The gas jet was turned up full, whistling steadily in its blue-tinted globe. Annie stood beneath the light, with her back to him.

'Say you're sorry.'

'I'm sorry.'

She turned to face him, her arms folded. 'Lick my feet. Go on, down on your knees.'

Breathless, he went down on the floor. One knee cracked a protest, and his neck was stiff.

He would be cured. Not long ago he had been assured of that. He wished he could remember where, and why he had been able to feel so confident about it.

Her hand was on his neck. With his head rammed against her shin he tugged clumsily at the buttons of his jacket. When she began to beat him he let himself go limp, submitting, relishing the pain, feeling it cleanse him and revive him after a night which had somehow frustrated his desire — a night when a promise had been dishonoured again.

At last, when the pain was too biting, he scrambled up and knocked the short riding-crop aside. She dodged skittishly away. Grabbing her, he pulled the shift over her head. She fought, laughing and spluttering within the folds of the garment. He tugged it down one arm and tossed it high in the air. It landed on the bowl of the gas jet.

He bore Annie down.

Suddenly there was a scorching pain down his back. Fire licked round his neck. He reared up and threw himself to one side. Annie's shift, ablaze from the jet, had fallen across his shoulders.

Convulsively he shrugged it from him on to the carpet. The flames curled out more eagerly. Annie was wriggling backwards on her knees, with her hands across her face as if the fire already threatened her eyes. Wentworth snatched his coat from the floor, threw it on the blaze, and jumped up and down on it. One tongue of flame licked out with playful venom at his bare leg and drew a shout of pain from him.

'Not yet!' he cried.

Annie's hands came away from her face. She made no sense of his words, but the sound shook her into action. She dashed out for a bucket of water and came back to throw it awkwardly, inaccurately, soaking Wentworth and the carpet as thoroughly as the coat and what was left of her shift.

They were silent, breathing hard.

'Not yet,' he whispered.

Annie gulped, and prodded the shreds on the floor with her foot.

'Well,' she said loudly and cheekily, 'you'll have to buy me a new one, won't you? An' I fancy one a lot fancier than that. For my birthday.'

Wentworth was picking up his clothes. 'Your birthday?' Along his forearm was more vivid, living colour where her riding-crop had raised a long weal. 'You told me you weren't even sure of your real name, so how can you know when you were born?'

'Oh, that was my mum. She said I was a Thursday child and I'd got far to go. Always said that, she did.'

Far to go, he thought: and me with you, me beside you along the way. It made him feel quite weak, and loving, and tearful.

'And she told me,' Annie went on with rare solemnity, giving due weight to one of the few facts she could cling to in her wayward life, 'she wasn't likely to forget the date 'cos it was the day after her own, and a day earlier and I'd have been a fine bloody birthday treat for her, wouldn't I? The 20th of June,' said Annie. 'That's what it was: the 20th of June.'

The acrid smell of burning made Wentworth want to sneeze. He went to the window and opened the sash so that air could blow in.

Bronwen said: 'You believe she really has been all those women we experienced, reincarnated over and over again, down the centuries?'

'I believe,' he corrected her, 'what I said early on — that she believes it.'

'But how . . . '

For a moment they were jostled apart by a couple of drunken revellers lurching from a tavern in the corner of the square. As one of them fell in the gutter, Caspian pushed the other aside and secured Bronwen's arm. Behind them was the Cavern of Mystery, which they had just left after appraising the performance of the new team of conjurors and illusionists assembled for the summer season. Ahead the Empire Theatre of Varieties sparkled with light and the haze of flowering shrubs along its veranda. A group of young men, led by one twirling a cane, hurried towards its entrance doors. Three young women in the shadow of an awning consulted one another, nodded, and followed them in.

Leicester Square reverberated with life. Men and women drove here, walked here, took their pick of theatre and magic and food and drink — and companionship. It was noisy and open and shameless. Far in time and space from the secret horrors of the Countess Báthory's cellars; or the single chair in the isolated temple folly on its little knoll.

Bronwen's head brushed her husband's shoulder. 'If it's all a personal fantasy, how could that woman have raised up such convincing spectres from the past?'

'She may have read widely, or been given a specialized education in history and legend.'

'And now believes she's ready for another reincarnation. Who's it to be this time?'

They stopped in a doorway while the tide of humanity rolled on across the square. Caspian said: 'Are we back to Elizabeth Relph again?'

'But if that were the pattern, then your guess at her being the catalyst in the alchemic formula is wrong. And so is our worry about her carrying that other personality within her. They can't all apply simultaneously.'

'Which makes Laura the likelier one. Chosen as the next host for this psychic parasite. Which could be why Elizabeth went to Nasmyth Lodge to claim her, either on instructions implanted in her mind — or for herself.'

'And why she has drawn even closer by engaging herself to marry the father?' added Bronwen unhappily.

'I wonder if that wedding is really destined ever to take place?'

The bustle of people moving to and fro was less immediate than the memory of two other unidentifiable people fleeing through a remoter, soundless night from Nasmyth Lodge. Bronwen struggled to keep them in perspective, but they taunted her and separated and vanished. 'I ought to have followed Elizabeth while you guarded Thornhill.'

'On my own I might not have been strong enough to protect him.'

'But if I'd followed Elizabeth and witnessed the moment of Ilona's emergence, I could have been close on her heels when she returned to Nasmyth Lodge.'

Ilona was no longer a dark cipher in an academic charade but an enemy who had encompassed their awareness with the flame of her hatred. 'She realized we were there, she may have grasped who we are. Will she hide from us now or search us out, to drive us out of her way?' They began to stroll again. As they turned down a quieter street Bronwen glanced back once at the blaze of light on the far side of Leicester Square. 'I think I preferred you as Count Caspar. One wave of the magic wand, a 'hey presto', and every knot was untied.'

'In that incarnation,' he said drily, 'the knots were of my own contrivance.'

His piercing whistle brought a hansom to the kerb. As they moved off, Bronwen asked: 'You think she'll try Thornhill again?'

'He must by now have moved out of the aspect for which he was chosen. She needs another Gemini, quickly. And there's still the fire element to be worked as well.' He frowned. 'I wonder what sign that indignant bookseller comes under?'

'The uninvited guest, that night?'

'Uninvited and unconventional. Hinde was right: it was a decidedly odd time to call with a grievance of that kind. Was he, too, summoned?'

'But the ritual wasn't ready for completion — for the final ceremony — that night.'

'No, but he may have had some part to play. He must belong in it somewhere. Perhaps I should call on him, sound him out.'

'He saw you,' said Bronwen. 'You were full in the light of the portico, right beside Hinde. He'd remember you and be on his guard. I saw him, but I doubt if he got much of a look at me: I was standing fairly well back, saying goodbye to Mrs. Dampier.'

'You can hardly go into an establishment of the kind he runs, if what Hinde says is true. Ladies have no cravings for such stimuli.'

'Indeed? Can you confirm that from personal experience, Doctor?'

Her mind teased his for the briefest instant.

'I hear you,' he said softly. 'Yes. That's how you are, and you're a poor dissembler. You wouldn't look convincing as a woman in need of leafing through suggestive books.'

They were approaching the Embankment. As they swung out and along the southern rim of Chelsea, she ventured: 'He might be less suspicious if I called to sell him something.'

★   ★   ★

Sir Andrew Thornhill was propped in one of his favourite positions, against the first-floor balcony rail of the Pantheon's spacious atrium. In one hand he held a glass; the other gesticulated to accompany the didactic boom of his voice. Hinde paused halfway up the staircase, but made himself continue, with every intention of striding past his brother-in-law.

'Aha, if it isn't Joseph. Haven't seen you for a week or so. Must be a week, isn't it?' Thornhill favoured his companion with a ponderous nod. 'Very lavish with the hospitality, old Joseph. Makes one's recollections very muddled, you know. Very muddled.' He belched an exaggerated laugh and then, catching Hinde's involuntary glance at the half-empty glass, became noticeably pink and bellicose. 'Don't worry, old fellow. Don't concern yourself. I'm not going to topple over and disgrace you.'

'I'm relieved to hear it.'

'A touch of indigestion that night, you know. Nothing to do with the wine.'

Hinde did not deign to reply but went in to take a brief luncheon on his own, choosing a corner table where he could read through a few Ministerial papers without interruption.

When he was ready to leave he went downstairs and along the passage to collect his coat.

The cloakroom door opened upon several parallel coat-racks. At their far end were two steps down to a tiled floor, with lavatories straight ahead and four wash-basins out of sight through a door on the left. Hinde had hung his coat on its usual peg, only a few feet from the steps. As he took it down he heard Thornhill's voice, amplified by the reverberations of the room beyond.

'I don't dare tell the poor unsuspecting innocent, of course. Have to leave him to find out for himself, poor devil.'

The answering murmur was discreet and inaudible.

'Oh, precious little doubt about it. Chap back from the Punjab. Knew the Relphs, said he'd always been sorry for the fellow. One of the conscientious types — worked hard while she was playing hard. Had all the young subalterns round her like flies. Sooner or later there was bound to be a scandal. Tried to hush it up, but didn't manage it too well by all accounts.' There was the thump and rattle of the wooden roller as Thornhill pulled at the towel. 'Up in the hills she carried on with some army officer on leave. Not the first by any means, but this one actually followed her from the local cantonment, leaving her poor blasted husband sweating away down there in the heat. Word got back to him. They say that's how he got killed — letting himself walk right into a spot of bother rather than endure any more of it when she got back from the hills.'

The other man must have turned towards the door. His voice was clearer now. 'He's your brother-in-law. Don't you owe him some sort of hint?'

'Can't do it. Let him find out for himself. Do him good. All those years younger than him, and with all that experience. A bit of a leaning towards that Indian stuff, I heard: you know, all those temple carvings and so on. Teach him a thing or two. God knows, he can do with it.'

Hinde hurried away with his coat over his arm before the two men could emerge and see what was in his face.

12

The original twelve photographs had been innocuous enough. The girl, though naked, had been posed in a series of decorous anatomical studies for the benefit of serious art students, and her grave expression suggested no indecent thoughts on her part or the possibility of any such in the mind of the viewer. Bronwen felt a creeping distaste at what she was now doing to the pictures. Several times in the course of these last few days she had been tempted to abandon the whole plan, which might in any case lead them nowhere.

She retouched the girl's mouth and painstakingly added shadows under the eyes in one picture, and enlarged a head, arm, and breast to produce a totally different impression from that of the full, formal pose. Reluctantly she was beginning to share the insidious fascination of the craftsman in pornography.

When she had finished she packed the resulting prints in her slim leather satchel and set off for Kemble Court.

The books in the shop window looked dreary rather than provocative. They had unadventurously geometric patterns on their covers, and only the suggestive titles offered an invitation to turn the pages.

Bronwen put a hand on the doorknob, shivered, and walked in. Above her a little bell swung wildly to and fro.

That night at Nasmyth Lodge she had seen Wentworth only from an angle, with odd glints of twilight and shadow on his face. Now, as he came through from the back of his shop, he was fleshier than she had thought, and rubbed his hands together as if caricaturing an unctuous clergyman. Then they separated and he set them solemnly on the counter, as a parson might have set his hands on the edge of his pulpit. His expression was forbidding. Ladies, as Caspian had predicted, were rarely among his customers.

'Yes, madam?'

'I was wondering,' she said, 'if you would be interested in purchasing some photographic studies on birthday themes.'

'This is not a stationer's, nor a picture gallery. I run a bookshop.'

'Quite so. But some of your clients might care to make up albums of the right sort of picture.'

Wentworth eyed her up and down suspiciously. 'You're from one of those women's busybody leagues?'

She unfastened the satchel and drew out the sheaf of twelve pictures, each mounted on thin card.

'I have taken the signs of the zodiac and prepared a birthday picture for each period. Here, for instance, is Virgo.'

She turned the print to face him. He stared down at it; then respectfully moved it aside and went on to the next, and the next.

'I see. Yes, I see, Miss . . . ?'

'Powys. Bronwen Powys. I have a photographic studio in South Audley Street.'

'Specializing in this kind of work?'

'Er . . . no. Not so far.' Bronwen lowered her gaze and picked shyly at the wooden edge of the counter. 'Business has not been too good lately. I thought I would experiment. There's a market for studies of this nature — isn't there?'

Wentworth snickered. 'A market for more advanced versions, yes. These are charming in their way. But there's a certain stiffness, a lack of . . . shall we say imagination?'

'I could try again, if — '

'I fancy modern requirements would be beyond you, young lady.'

Still his gaze lingered on the picture in which Bronwen had blended exposures in an interplay of two phantom bodies.

'That's my own birth sign,' she said. 'I thought it was rather ingenious.'

He glanced at the handwritten legend on the mount.

'Gemini.'

'In my case, the 19th of June. All of twenty-seven years ago, I'm afraid,' she added deprecatingly but distinctly; and went on with new boldness: 'My main difficulty has been finding models without undue shyness. So few are prepared to abandon themselves to the true flow of the picture.'

He sucked in his lip. Turning over three

more prints he came to the last in the pile. Over the head of the seated girl Bronwen had touched in a fine-meshed veil, falling to her creamy shoulders. 'I see. Yes. Your ideas are interesting, but I agree about your model. If you wished to pursue your studies more fruitfully . . . '

This time he looked Bronwen up and down as if envisaging her in one of her own photographic poses. And this time he did not look away.

'Have you any advice to offer?'

'I might find some young women who wouldn't be too inhibited in their response to your — ah — aesthetic ideals.'

'I'd be glad to have the chance of working with them.'

Wentworth's attention returned to the picture of the veiled girl. 'What led you to devise this one?'

'I felt an affinity with the theme: the abnegation of personality, leaving only the physical essence.'

Wentworth frowned like a man puzzled by some resemblance, which eluded him, trying in spite of the shrouded features to identify a half-familiar face.

There was a chilly draught as if the shop door had opened to admit a customer. Someone sidled between Bronwen and Wentworth and chuckled approval of the photographs. So close, one almost felt the breathing; and an arm seemed to lie lightly but possessively on Bronwen's shoulder. But the door remained shut, and there was nobody there.

Wentworth glanced uneasily sideways, then stooped to tug a heavy package from beneath the counter. Untying a knot with parsimonious care he pulled back string and wrapping paper. Down one side of the parcel was scrawled in thick crayon what might have been Mindor St. or Minton St.

He took out a volume and opened it in front of Bronwen.

She contemplated twisted faces and chains, phallic batons and other banal accoutrements. Thanks to her own recent absorption in the sheer technicalities of such photography and printing she was able to maintain an unblushing detachment.

'Given the right co-operation,' she said blandly, 'I'd be ashamed not to produce more stimulating work than that.'

Wentworth tapped her selection of prints together with epicene fingers. Then he began edging her towards the door. 'I'll be in touch as soon as I've found fully qualified participants.'

She handed him the business card of the Powys Photographing and Enlarging Studio. 'I'll look forward to hearing from you.'

Silent laughter echoed as in an empty church. Sickeningly, Bronwen felt she was known and recognized, that the ageless spirit was so sure of itself that it no longer needed to hide. It taunted her, anticipating her plans, making a mock of them. Fear clutched at her stomach. She fought it off. If Ilona was really gathering strength, so would Bronwen be strong in herself and in Caspian. Soon, somehow, there must be a meeting; and that would be no time for weakness.

Feet shuffled faintly on the other side of the counter. From the inner doorway a girl, bare arms akimbo, stared at Bronwen with smouldering, jealous eyes.

The bell tolled high and tinny as

Wentworth held the shop door open. 'We'll be doing business together soon, Miss Powys. Very soon. I feel it in my bones.'

★ ★ ★

Caspian passed his card across the desk in the musty little office. It was the one that announced him in florid type as Count Caspar, Master of Prestidigitation and Illusion, of the Cavern of Mystery, Leicester Square.

The man on the other side of the desk was identified to the outside world as Walter Dingley by chipped gilt lettering on the window behind his head.

'Count Caspar? Know the name well, sir, who doesn't? And what can I do for you?'

'I'm looking for warehouse space in the neighbourhood. We're negotiating a regular half-hour of magic in the Bedford Music Hall programme round the corner, and we don't want to be transporting scenery and equipment to and fro all the time. I will need somewhere secure against those who'd steal our secrets as readily as our props!'

'Got just the very thing. A yard with a couple of nice big sheds, not a stone's throw from the Bedford.'

'I did see your sign outside a place in Minton Street.'

Caspian had found Minton Street a short distance to the east of Camden Square. On the crown of the hill a new red and yellow brick church set the tone for the terraces curving smugly away below. The only break on one side of the street was made by two rusted iron gates opening on to a patch of dried-up grass, bisected by a tiled path leading to the south door of a high, narrow chapel. Finding the gates unfastened, Caspian walked up the path; but the oak door would not open.

Behind the nearer houses ran a high brick wall, as if the owners wished to shut out this sombre relic of a rural past. Where one would have expected to find a church notice board was a sign declaring:

PRIVATE PROPERTY
DINGLEY'S WAREHOUSING
TRESPASSERS WILL BE PROSECUTED

Mr. Dingley's office proved to be no great distance from that of Mr. Noakes and the Camden Lecture Rooms. Caspian did not suppose the two gentlemen and the caretaker would ever have had cause to compare notes; or that, had they done so, they would have been struck by anything significant.

For himself he felt that, if he could properly interpret what was now within his grasp, he would be close to spanning another gap in the charade.

'You mean the old chapel?' Dingley was saying.

'Deconsecrated some while ago, I'd imagine.'

'Oh, quite some time, yes. No call for it any more. But it's been quite a blessing to me, you might say.'

'From outside the proportions of the building seem most suitable for my requirements.'

'Well, it's taken at the moment. Been let this last year and more. A very respectable tenant. An antiquarian bookseller,' added Mr. Dingley, letting some of the prestige of such a profession rub off on him. 'From a very good part of town.'

'Keeping his stocks this far out?'

'There's not that much space in the heart of it, you know. And what there is, well, it costs a pretty penny. Besides, with all the thievery and roguery there is these days, and him with all those priceless old books, it's wise to keep as much as possible well out of the way, up here where it's safe.'

'I quite appreciate his concern. Very wise, as you say.'

'Not many would think to come looking for his sort of book up here.'

'No,' said Caspian, 'they wouldn't. Your bookseller friend must have a vast stock, to occupy all that space.'

'Oh, he doesn't fill the chapel. Nowhere near it.'

'So there'd be room enough for someone else to share.'

'I did have someone else using one end of it, once. But he was slow on his rent, and Mr. Wentworth complained there'd been some pilfering.'

'Wentworth? That would be the bookseller?'

'Oh, now, he wouldn't want me to go round telling everyone. Letting it out like that.'

'I wouldn't dream of breaking a professional confidence,' Caspian assured him.

'Well, I don't know. You do seem very set on the place, sir.'

'It's a pity not to use your resources to the full, don't you think? Increased income with no increase of trouble. Mr. Wentworth and I have much in common: neither of us wants valuable stock at the mercy of intruders. We could probably come to some mutual agreement about precautions against burglars, thereby safeguarding your property even more efficiently, Mr. Dingley.'

Mr. Dingley was beginning to succumb. 'I'm not saying I could accommodate you, Count, but there'd be no harm in me having a word with Mr . . . with my other client . . . and seeing how he took it.'

'Splendid. And now, if I might have an opportunity of inspecting the interior?'

Mr. Dingley hesitated. 'I keep keys of my own, naturally. But if anything did go astray, I wouldn't want Mr. Wentworth to

300

think for a minute — '

'I'm sure he wouldn't. And for my part, I solemnly swear not to abstract any of his incunabula.'

'I wouldn't know where to look for that, I'm sure.'

They walked round to Minton Street, and Mr. Dingley unlocked the chapel door.

Caspian paced slowly up the aisle.

The doors and backs of the box-pews were higher than any he had ever seen. It was a marvel that those members of the congregation who sat to the back of the nave could see anything at all, save when the preacher was up in the pulpit. Today those rear pews acted as cupboards: squared-up heaps of what must be Mr. Wentworth's books were stacked on the floor and the benches within, most of them covered over with tarpaulin. Caspian longed to lift a corner of canvas and see just what dubious treasures Wentworth was hiding away.

He reached the front pews, which were empty. They were not as dusty as might have been expected; and when he turned towards the pulpit, the steps looked as if they might have been cleaned not so very long ago.

'There are never any services held here — private services, or anything of that kind?'

Dingley snorted. 'In the middle of all this?' He waved at the tarpaulins, the grimed glass of the windows, and the shreds of carpet on two shadowed steps. 'Not what you'd call a very holy setting, not any more.'

There was indeed no atmosphere either of sanctity or of desecration. All resonances of joyful or fearful worship had been damped down. Caspian, striving to capture some intimation of those who must have congregated here recently, was left in a vacuum.

Mr. Dingley showed him out and locked the door behind them.

'Wentworth's the only other one with a key,' Caspian reported when he got home. 'It must be through him that Ilona makes all her dispositions, whether he's conscious of it or not.'

Merely by naming her aloud he seemed to be inviting her closer.

She must by now be growing desperate.

Caspian went on: 'Through Wentworth she gained access to the chapel. She implanted in him dates and procedures so that he's not really aware of what he's doing or of what she intends. Possibly she meets him more frequently than the others; or at least meets him on a plane of greater intensity where she can exercise her full mesmeric influence over him.'

'He's her stage manager.'

'And general messenger boy. As when he preceded her to Nasmyth Lodge that night, to set things in motion with Thornhill. Things,' he said, 'which we frustrated.'

'And now he may unknowingly transmit my birth date to her,' said Bronwen. 'My supposed birth date, that is.'

'That's something I'm not happy about.'

'As long as you're with me, I'll be safe.'

'She may already have guessed.'

Laughing at me, thought Bronwen. Laughing at both of us. But she said: 'It's our best chance. We have to tempt her out into the open. And she'll have to react somehow to what we're letting her believe.'

'She has been strong-willed enough to dominate all those others. If she fancies claiming you as well, there's no telling which direction she'll strike from.'

'We must be ready for her,' said Bronwen steadily.

★ ★ ★

The table and two rustic chairs on the terrace had been gathered into the afternoon shadow of the west wing. Elizabeth moved one chair back into the sunlight. Hinde stood contemplating the tableau she made against the open window.

She said: 'You're very solemn today, Joseph.'

'I'm sorry. Rather too many things on my mind.'

Lightly she rested her fingertips on the chair. 'Come and sit here. Then I can decide whether you will be best placed for Mrs. Caspian's camera next Thursday. If we can rely on such sun, the results should be admirable. If you will allow yourself to smile!'

He tried to walk to the chair, but found himself hesitating by the table.

'Let's leave the posing to Mrs. Caspian when the time comes. She'll know what looks most suitable.'

Her hand remained where it was but he saw the knuckles whiten as she gripped the bar more tightly.

She said: 'There's something wrong.'

'Things on my mind. You'll get used to my peculiar moods.'

'Perhaps you don't want me to get used to them?'

He evaded the challenge. 'I'll endeavour to keep them to a minimum. But affairs of state do persist in darkening one's outlook.'

'You're a poor liar,' she said flatly. Her slender neck was erect, her head was proud. 'Joseph, what has been said to you?'

'My dear, whatever are we talking about?'

'That's what I think you'd better tell me.'

'The whole matter's so vague. I should

305

never have given it a second thought.'

'No, that won't do.' She gripped the chair yet more tightly. 'You've met someone — from India?'

'I've ... heard of someone. In a roundabout way. So that neither of us should pay a moment's heed — '

'Someone,' she said, 'who has revived the gossip which plagued me there.'

'Your past is your concern and not mine, my dearest. Our life began when you came to Laura's rescue, and that's as good a place to start as any.'

'You'll always be wondering. You won't be able to help yourself.'

'We're to be married. Nothing makes any difference to that. It will all go ahead as planned — '

'As a matter of honour?' she said frigidly.

'You did me the honour of consenting to marry me — '

'Joseph, if you think I'll marry you simply because you're too noble and self-righteous to disown a contract — oh, no, I'll not have that! For if you were so correct, and it all turned out as before, only even colder

. . . oh, no, please God, no.'

He despised himself for having let his fretful jealousy show through.

'Turned out as before?' He tried to pick up the thread of what she had been talking about.

'I should have told you everything, weeks ago.'

'I prefer you not to torment yourself.'

'You'll only imagine things ten times worse than they are. And really there's so little to tell, which makes it all the more difficult to make convincing denials.'

She came round the chair and sat in it, carefully resting her left arm on the lumpy woodwork. 'My husband was a . . . a twisted man. Twisted in some way, which made it impossible for me to help him. Or to love him.' Her voice was as steady as her arm. 'I married him because my parents and everyone else made it clear that in India there was no other future for a girl. You accepted a suitable man, you helped him in his career, provided him with two children — two were regarded as most proper in those circumstances — and you took your prescribed place at the prescribed dinners and the prescribed parties. And if, after the wedding, you found a secret self within you that found married life not to her taste, you kept her truly secret. You lived according to the rules. If I did nothing else, I did that.

'Yet within months my husband was accusing me of being involved with other men. When I wanted to continue studying the religions of the country he forbade it because such eccentricities would damage his prospects of promotion — and because I was using it only as a pretext for a relationship with an Indian. Then there was a young captain who behaved outrageously when my husband was present, and even more outrageously when he was away. Once I had to drive him from the bungalow, and a dozen different stories circulated on that score. Then when I was up in Chakrata with other wives during the monsoon season, there were scores of flirtations and near flirtations; and the more I held myself aloof, the more it was whispered that I had assignations of a much more serious nature. That same captain took his leave while I was in Chakrata and pursued me there. And that was when we heard my husband had died.'

'Because he'd heard misleading reports?'

'So you've been favoured with that version?' said Elizabeth bitterly. 'Much more likely he'd been drinking, and grew aggressive and blundered into a quarrel of his own making. But the popular story put the blame on me. I was shunned — except by men who thought that now I'd hold out no longer against them. My parents and husband were dead, I was alone, I ought to welcome protection. There were plenty of them willing to 'look after Eliza' as I heard it put.' In the warm sunlight she shivered. 'I hated them all. Worst of all, even after he was dead and I kept asking myself if somehow our life couldn't have been different, I hated my husband.'

'If he'd been any kind of man, surely he would have driven the others away. A true husband — '

'That he never was.' Her free hand rose to her breast, pressing against some old pain there. 'Humiliating me, showing himself incapable and then blaming me for . . . for . . . No, it's all too close, I've no right to expect you . . . ' Harshly, in a rush, she went on: 'Our marriage was never a marriage. He grovelled, he tried, he cursed himself and he cursed me. It was shaming. I wanted to cry. Night after night I wanted to cry. But he was the one who cried. And to make up for it, he boasted to his cronies about his capabilities as a . . . a lover.' The word cracked out as the worst of insults. 'And about me, and what I was like. And then reviled me, when he was in his cups, as a faithless slut — and so excited the imaginations of those others.'

'If you *had* turned for happiness to another — '

'I turned to nobody. And I encouraged none to come after me. Yet they wouldn't keep away. It was as if they knew something about me which I didn't want to admit to myself. They were waiting for this other person to come out, so that they could pounce. But I'd nothing to give them. Perhaps I've nothing to give anyone.'

Her head sank. She was spent.

Hinde said shakily: 'It will be different this time. I swear it.' His hand under her chin tilted it up and held it. Her eyes searched his.

'Will it? There'll always be someone to remember, or misremember, and spread old slanders'

'I'll show you — and them — how little that matters.'

She stood up so that he had to step away from her. 'I wasn't ready for marriage,' she said. 'Not then. I tried. But if one has to try, how can it be love? How can it even be companionship?'

'When you walked into my house — '

'When I was carried into your house,' — she laughed at this bright flash of memory — 'I knew so soon what I wanted. It was so soon; so frightening. It would shock you if I told you.'

'Tell me.'

'No woman fit to become Mrs. Joseph Hinde would speak so brazenly. Can you see me as your wife, as the fit companion for the most upright Minister, the preacher of moral standards, the crusader — '

'Don't mock me.'

'Joseph!' It was a stricken cry. 'I'm not mocking you. I'm trying to make you see, for your own sake . . . that you must release me.'

She tried to move away from the chair. He stood his ground, so that she walked into his arms. He held her, and his breath quickened in time with hers.

He said: 'We've both waited too long.'

'And now it's too late. I'll always be afraid, now. To be unable to help my husband, to bring about nothing but disgust in both of us — do you think I could face that again? With you? You whom I love. I love you, but I've nothing to give. Nothing left, Joseph.'

'Nothing left? I'll prove you wrong. I'll prove it now, and put an end to your nonsense.'

'Joseph, I'll make you unhappy. I should never have agreed, should never have let myself dream . . . You must listen to me.'

'Only when you say what I wish to hear.'

He was forcing her into the house, laughing, shaken by his own laughter. She gasped and shook her head, and was saying 'No, no,' but beginning to laugh with him. 'Joseph, if I have to lose you now . . . if I'm . . . taken . . . '

'Who'll try taking you from me?'

The swooning of her body against his side, the sweetly trembling response too overwhelming for her to hide, the scent and breath and movement of her were all such that he scarcely heard or wanted to make sense of her reply.

'The one who sent me here in the first place.'

He drew her closer.

'Joseph, she shan't have me.' She was weeping, and her lips stammered uncontrollably. 'She shan't, wherever she is.'

★　★　★

She sat in her dark seclusion, her whole self dormant. Then self-awareness returned like the slow suffusion of a dawn sky. Thoughts stirred, her appetite sharpened.

And her anger.

They were slipping through her fingers. The chosen successor, already snatched back into the insipid sunlight of her pathetic, conventional world, never knowing what riches she had missed. The air ritual collapsing, leaving a gap in the formula. And now the sacrificial catalyst in danger of forsaking her. She could not wait, could not painstakingly search out the elements under new signs and in new bodies, delicately reconstructing the whole process from the start. This present ritual must be completed. Time was running out.

The Caspian man and woman had trespassed and fragmented the circle. And the woman was venturing again. If she came within range this time, if she dared . . .

No, there must be no anger. Anger was too potent a distraction. There was too much at stake. Eternity at stake.

Joy awoke suddenly: a malicious joy, which added a harsh savour to the appetite.

The Caspian woman was fumbling her way towards the old Ilona. Very well. She should feel the birth pangs of the new Ilona.

13

'Many happy returns of the day, Miss Powys.'

Bronwen had not heard the outer door open, and the oily little chuckle took her unawares. She almost dropped a set of stereoscopic slides, which she had been slotting into the corner cabinet. Prodding them safely into place she turned to face the man who had soundlessly come to the desk on which her appointments book lay open.

'I wasn't expecting you.'

'No, Miss Powys?' Wentworth's lips pulled back from his teeth. 'But I told you we'd soon be doing business together. What more appropriate day to start?'

'You've got a good memory for dates.'

'And for the inventive illustrations which go with them.'

Bronwen glanced over the frosted lower section of the studio window. A small boxed-in delivery van waited outside.

'Yes,' said Wentworth. 'I think I've arranged a satisfactory sitting. Though naturally our subjects will not be seated for any great part of the time. We'll expect something more energetic than that.'

Bronwen made a show of turning over a page of the book. Her wedding ring glinted, and she let her left hand rest under the page while she slid the ring off and transferred it as unobtrusively as possible to her apron pocket.

'You want us to settle on a date now? And you'll let me know the exact location?'

'I want you to come with me at this moment,' he said, 'to the excellent place I've selected.'

'But I wasn't expecting you. Nothing's prepared.'

'I'm sure it won't take you a few minutes to assemble the necessary paraphernalia. But please let us not delay too long.'

'If you'd given me reasonable notice — '

'We have to seize what opportunities present themselves.'

His buttery complexion, with streaks and blotches of darker hue caught in it, gave him a sluggish, bilious appearance. One felt it would take only a push or a harsh word to make him crumple moistly in on himself. Yet at the same time he was implacable. His pouched eyes were dead, and he smiled a dead, fixed smile that took it for granted that she would not reject the invitation. Invitation — or command.

Somewhere that woman was waiting. There had been no time for her to coach and indoctrinate Bronwen as the other recruits had been indoctrinated. Was she intending to start today? She must have been impatient, to have risked sending her messenger with such a direct summons: impatient or hideously confident.

'I can't just close the studio in the middle of the afternoon,' Bronwen temporized.

'We'll not get another opportunity like this one.' The fingers of Wentworth's right hand crawled under a page of the appointments book like an insect probing its way round the underside. A page flipped back. 'You've no bookings for the rest of the day.'

An unspoken invitation curled around

Bronwen's mind as clammily as those creeping fingers, luring her from the studio into the unknown.

Of course she must go. If she missed this chance they might lose any hope of reaching Ilona in time to avert further deaths.

But there must be a way of calling Alexander to follow.

Bronwen turned towards the curtain behind which she kept two small cameras and slide-boxes, spinning out the minutes. She could not risk a telepathic message. It stood little chance of winging true across the distance between them; and such an exhausting cry would by its very fervour jar the attention of Ilona and her emissary.

Wentworth followed her into the darkroom.

'I see you lack for nothing in the way of modem equipment, Miss Powys. You are obviously prepared for any professional challenge.'

Smothered by his nearness and his rancid smell, she slipped the hook on to the door so that it would not swing shut.

Caspian was miles away, far too many miles away.

They had agreed they must be mutually ready for Ilona if and when she prowled into action. For more than a week they had kept close together during working hours, though not so close that Miss Powys would be seen by a malevolent observer as Mrs. Caspian. She arrived at the studio alone and left alone. Driving home, she took circuitous routes and checked at various junctions whether she was being followed. There was no hint of a pursuer. Any determined enquirer could have traced her and confirmed that she was married: it was no secret, and could have been verified through any number of business and social channels. What they could not estimate was how determined the Ilona-self was, how wary she was, and through what channels she would work. It might be that she had guessed too much already and was biding her time rather than theirs. It was a risk: just one of many.

They must not risk drifting too far apart.

The days moved past. Nobody invaded their dreams or their waking lives.

Caspian pored over an ephemeris to establish the ruling conjunctions of Bronwen's fictitious birth date and from them estimate the most dangerous days between now and the end of the Gemini period. Even if the date had been authentic, Ilona could not have divined the precise hour of Bronwen's birth, so all her other mystical calculations would be hampered; but even from a general assessment there were indications of two particular days being markedly more favourable than the rest.

They lived through the first of those two days with their shared mind poised and tense, like a hunter with finger a hair's breadth from the trigger in case the prey should spring without warning from the undergrowth. The strain of keeping unfalteringly alert was exhausting: taut readiness for the faintest rustle or flicker of movement, and at the same time iron control to ensure that the quarry's attention was not too sharply drawn to their presence. At the end of the twenty-four hours Bronwen drew back the curtains and looked out on the grey morning sheen of the Thames and on shrouded hulks cowering under the far bank. Her drained sensibilities were in a state to conceive hideous monsters out of the interplay of mist and reflected light. She felt Caspian slacken and fall wearily away from her. Before she could cry out her desolation his mind was sunk in hers again, tired but gentle and reassuring.

'Rest, my love. If she hopes to wear us down, we'll not let her.'

On the second crucial day they endured the same torment of apprehension, with the same result. Again there was no whisper of Ilona.

'Either she has given up and intends to frame a whole new sequence when conditions are favourable,' theorized Caspian, 'or she has picked out somebody else for the air symbol.'

He could not disguise his instinctive relief that Bronwen's sly challenge had not been taken up. But nor could he disguise from her his concern about some other substitute victim, unknown and beyond their reach.

'We've frightened her off,' said Bronwen, 'and she's after somebody else — somebody with far less power of resistance than we two.'

Without touching her he was clasping her hand in his. Tacitly they both understood that they could not stand aside now. It was impossible to keep at a peak of full alertness, like a sentry unblinking and ready to fire in a split second; but they must put out antennae, leave themselves open to the slightest tremor of an approaching storm.

Caspian dismissed Bronwen's supposed birthday itself as a date reproducing few of the aspects that would best serve the woman's alchemic formula. Insensibly, though still receptive, they eased their rigorous liaison. On the 19th of June Caspian announced that he would allow himself to go farther afield. There was to be a theatrical and music hall managers' luncheon at the Crystal Palace out at Sydenham, when the expansion of entertainment in the grounds there was to be debated. It was known that the master

John Nevil Maskelyne intended to put forward some ambitious suggestions; and the absence of Count Caspar would undoubtedly have attracted unfavourable comment.

'I shall be only a few hours. Then we must contrive some plan for approaching that woman from another direction, and finding who else may have fluttered into her web.'

The problem occupied Bronwen's mind that day as she indexed and stowed away recent sequences of prints and slides. Her first plan had misfired: she took this so much for granted that five minutes after Wentworth's arrival in the studio she still could not believe that Ilona was really taking the bait.

She had picked on a fortuitous moment to send her messenger.

Or else she had foreseen every move and had been slyly waiting for Bronwen to be taken off guard. It was Ilona, not they, who had chosen the time for confrontation.

Bronwen completed her hesitant preparations with Wentworth at her shoulder.

She wondered how long it would take Alexander to discover that she had gone. He might go straight home and not be aware of her absence until early evening.

She must leave a message. But Wentworth had her under observation the whole time.

Pulling the set of zodiacal prints from a drawer, she fanned them out. 'Shall we take these for reference?'

'Gracious, no. I'm relying on you to produce something in a much more adventurous vein.'

Bronwen pushed the photographs to one side, managing to flick the Gemini subject well clear of the others. Her hand rested on it, as she willed all her love and need for Alexander down through her fingertips, straining to leave a message that would reverberate until he got here.

Wentworth helped to carry the camera, tripod, plate wallet and magnesium flash box out to the street. When these were stowed in the van he handed Bronwen up to the seat at the front, and settled on the driver's seat beside her.

The time was here. The enemy was

waiting. But did the enemy recognize her as such, or merely as an innocent victim?

Bronwen felt calm now. She would not falter. She was alone yet, even with Caspian out of reach, not alone. They had known and been so much together, he and she, that in peril he would always be with her.

I love, and am loved. So who can destroy me?

Still she longed for him to pick up the trail and be with her in the flesh.

'Quite comfortable?' Wentworth turned to smirk at her.

She tried to fix in her mind, as she would have fixed the scenes on photographic plates, each scene and turning they took. But there were so many doublings back and forth, and so many terraces all alike, that she lost track.

At last they began to toil up a hill, and came to a halt before a pair of gates. Wentworth got down to open them, and led the horse and van round the back of a begrimed chapel, the animal having to pick its way over shreds of rubble and tufts of weed. They stopped close to a door surmounted by a brick crescent, mimicking a Norman arch. Wentworth fitted a key into the lock. He pushed the door open and waved Bronwen in.

'Leave the equipment to me.'

She stepped into a high, narrow room, made narrower by a wooden partition, which cut off one segment. Through a gap in the planking she saw a couple of small chairs, Sunday school size, one tipping over on a broken leg. Behind her the door closed and she heard the key turn in the lock again.

'My camera. You said you'd — '

'We won't need it immediately.'

'But I'll need to set it up — '

'Let me show you the scene first. I'll give you a chance to assess what you're dealing with.'

He shepherded her across the vestry and on into the musty nave.

A small figure was crouching at the west end of the aisle. A dark wing dangled above her head, like a predatory bird choosing its moment to descend on a scurrying insect. Light from a window behind Bronwen broke over the high, irregular surrounds of the front pews, picking out dust on one corner, gleaming in a brass latch, its beam filling and swirling with dust motes. As she became used to the light and shade she saw that the dark wing beyond was a loose end of tarpaulin, pulled away from a tall stack of books. The little urchin scuttling from side to side, stooping and straightening up, was tearing books and periodicals into separate leaves and scattering them over the floor and into the pews.

Wentworth's voice rang hollow along the aisle. 'Whatever d'you think you're doing, Annie?'

The girl stood up and wiped a strand of hair from her eyes. 'You told me to, before you left.' She eyed Bronwen with impertinent curiosity, souring into the jealousy she had shown that earlier day in Wentworth's shop.

'Did I?' For the first time this afternoon Wentworth sounded uncertain. 'If you say so, well, yes, then I suppose I could have done.' He stood beside Bronwen. 'They say my books are fit only for burning. Want to drive me out of business, some of our friends in Westminster. D'you think we ought to save them the trouble and burn the whole lot here, on the spot?'

He barred her only escape. There was no room for her to run, if she had been minded to, between the column by his right arm and the curve of the pulpit steps.

In turning her head to explore the gloomy interior she caught a glimpse of colour and the slightest movement in one of the front pews. A woman sat there, waiting, only her head and shoulders visible.

Bronwen took a step up the aisle. Wentworth stood to one side with exaggerated courtesy, but still blocked her retreat. She went on a few paces and looked over the door into the pew.

Elizabeth Relph stared expressionlessly back at her.

★   ★   ★

Joseph Hinde rattled the handle of the door in South Audley Street. Certain of Elizabeth's intention to come here, he could not believe the studio was closed and unoccupied. Irritably he turned irritably away. If the two women had gone together to Cheyne Walk, or if Elizabeth had gone there in the first place, then he would make his way there.

Before he could leave, a carriage slowed in to the kerb, and Alexander Caspian descended.

'Mr. Hinde.' Caspian was flushed and in convivial mood. 'Come to make final arrangements for another set of souvenir portraits?'

He sauntered to the door, and turned the handle.

'There's nobody there,' said Hinde.

'At this time of day?' Caspian took out a ring of keys and with some hesitation selected one.

Hinde said: 'I was hoping to find Mrs. Relph here.'

'You'd made an appointment — and Bron's not even here to open the door?'

'I had a feeling Mrs. Relph was hurrying here to cancel an appointment we'd made.'

Caspian turned the key and stood back

so that Hinde could enter. It was quiet in the studio, the sounds of the street muffled.

'You're worried about something,' said Caspian. His joviality grated on Hinde's frayed nerves. 'My dear chap, do sit down. No, not on that bench: Bronwen favours that for funerals and solemn clerical portraits. You know — parting gifts for departing vicars.'

'As Mrs. Relph isn't here, I'll take my leave.'

'She may have been here and coaxed my wife into taking tea with her. They're probably in the corner of some expensive tearoom exchanging gossip and denigrating the two of us. Or Bron is talking her out of cancelling your sitting, if that *is* what brought her here.'

'I can't think where else she might have gone, looking as she did.'

'And how did she look, then?' Caspian was humming to himself unconcernedly, strolling about the room. 'My dear sir, a girl is entitled to a few doubts and changes of mind as her wedding day approaches. You must be patient.'

'She looked as my daughter looked when she drew away from me that time,' said Hinde: 'purposeful . . . and utterly indifferent towards me.'

Caspian's bonhomie faded. He came to a standstill; and the jaunty humming died away.

'You'd had a difference of opinion?' It was as though Caspian insisted on hearing that this was all it amounted to.

'None at all.'

On the contrary, thought Hinde wretchedly. Very much to the contrary. Hadn't she abandoned herself as impulsively and wildly as he, hadn't she been as prodigal and unstinting, crying her long cry of delight and then sharing that long companionable drowsiness of satiety? He had been shaken, overturned, unleashed into wild places he had never known. And then together they had been tranquil in a way he had never known.

Yet now she had turned and gone, blank-faced, away from him.

I sinned, he said to himself. He had said it a dozen times on his way here, as the old commandments laid their stern yoke on his shoulders again. I drew her into sin, and exulted in it, and now she's ashamed and I have the price to pay.

'You must tell me,' Caspian urged. 'It's imperative. When did she set out?'

'An hour or so ago. We'd been talking, making plans, discussing the sitting we'd arranged with your wife, and laughing over some silly joke about it.' The change from laughter to bleak repudiation had been terrifying. 'Then she seemed to have second thoughts. As if she'd remembered past disappointments . . . disillusionment. That fixed look came into her eyes, and she said she had an appointment and must go and . . . and settle things.'

'What things?'

'That was all she'd say. I might have ceased to exist. But we'd just been talking about Mrs. Caspian and the pictures we'd commissioned, and I thought she must have come here. Now I suppose — oh, I suppose she may have gone to her rooms. To pack, or . . . settle whatever it is she has in mind . . . '

He could guess at neither the reasons nor the outcome.

Caspian said: 'She didn't look like that on the night when you announced your engagement, even when Thornhill was in danger.'

'Why should she? Thornhill had nothing to do with her. She was upset for a while, as we all were by that deplorable exhibition, but — '

'She wasn't summoned that night. Because it wasn't the final ceremony, and she had no part to play in Thornhill's sacrifice. Or because' — Caspian flinched — 'oh, God, Bronwen must have been right: we should have split up and watched both of them.'

'I see there's no point in my troubling you further. I shouldn't have assumed so readily — '

'She wasn't among those summoned away,' said Caspian fiercely, 'because within her is the one who gives the commands. She was conveniently there at your house that night, and nicely and neatly all the rest of them assembled there just as she ordered. And when the first attempt went awry, she drove off and returned for another attempt. Today the meeting's elsewhere, so she has gone. And so has my wife.'

He pounded the top of the long filing cabinet, disturbing a pile of prints. One slithered away from the others. Caspian stared at it.

Hinde was taken aback. It would never have occurred to him that Mrs. Caspian traded in such deplorable material. Nor that Caspian could have been attracted by the suggestiveness of that veiled head above the naked body. On the card of the mount, gilt letters spelled out a word: Gemini.

Caspian touched the picture, and started as if he had been stung. Then he forced his hand carefully down again.

'My darling,' he murmured. 'Yes, my darling. Hold on. *Please* . . . be strong.'

Without warning he was on his way to the back of the premises. Hinde hurried to catch him up. 'You know where Elizabeth's to be found?'

'I think I know where they're both to be found.'

'My carriage is at the front.'

'Then drive home in it, and stay there, and pray.'

Caspian went out into a cobbled alley and on across the mews. He wrenched at a stable door and grated it open.

'I'm coming with you,' said Hinde.

'You won't like what you see.'

'Elizabeth — '

'May be playing another part today. Not one you'll care for.'

★ ★ ★

Bronwen shook the door of the pew but the latch refused to budge. Elizabeth made no move either to let her in or to wave her away.

Bronwen said: 'Mrs. Relph. Elizabeth. Listen to me. Please listen. Don't let yourself be swamped by that other one. I'm talking to you, to you — to the real you.'

There was not so much as the tremor of an eyelid.

The girl Annie, still scattering pages on all sides, edged along the aisle on her knees. 'Who you going on at?'

'Very well,' cried Bronwen. 'If I have to talk to the other one, very well. You ordered me to be brought here, you shall listen. Listen! You're wasting your time. Do you hear me? Wasting your time. The game can't be played out your way: the pieces no longer fit.'

Wentworth's footsteps shuffled away behind her. Annie got to her feet and went back for another package of leaflets, which she began to rip open. She was beginning to enjoy the rhythm of tearing and destroying.

'Even if you'd had the time' — Bronwen hammered it home — 'it wouldn't have succeeded with me. You could never have indoctrinated me. You've chosen the wrong person.'

'I don't think so, Mrs. Caspian.'

The voice was not Elizabeth's but a deep contralto from behind Bronwen: behind and above. She turned and saw nothing. Then she raised her eyes.

A veiled figure stood motionless in the pulpit.

Annie let out a little squeak.

Elizabeth had risen reverently to her feet and was yearning up at that shrouded figure. Light from the east window touched the dark head with a steely halo.

'Whoever you are,' said Bronwen, 'you've misjudged the whole thing.'

'I don't think you need to ask who I am, Mrs. Caspian.'

'My name — '

'Is Caspian. Wife of the amateur magician.' The adjective came out scathingly.

'And *your* real name?' Bronwen made herself ask. 'Let's have an end to this perverse hide-and-seek. Who are you? Show yourself.'

Two hands went up to the veil. Bronwen had seen the hands before — the androgynous fingers, which had once tapped her set of prints into fussy neatness, and now were delicately lifting the veil. The hands of Edgar Wentworth.

And the face of Edgar Wentworth.

Yet not his face. As she watched, it sagged in on itself like softening mud, shifting into new contours. Wentworth fought to remain Wentworth; then let himself be taken over by an older face, incredibly older, ravaged by some terrible long drawn-out knowledge of the unknowable.

Annie edged her way along the end of

the pews until she was beside Bronwen. 'Is this another of your games?'

A younger woman's features strove to assert themselves through the decay of a dozen incarnations, and then itself dissolved into the putrescence of an age which was more than mere physical age. The bony framework of Wentworth's skull was still there, holding necrosis in check — but precariously, flimsily, too close to melting away into an ultimate deliquescence.

'I am Ilona.'

Annie went down on all fours and began to yelp like a terrified puppy.

14

They talked in bursts of unfinished sentences, often at cross-purposes. Words were part of the nervous exertion, which drove the horse and gig on.

'This neighbourhood.' Hinde looked out with mounting foreboding. 'You're sure you know where we're heading?'

Tentatively Caspian opened his mind to the frenzy of thoughts endlessly raging through the ether. Out of the turmoil he wanted to hear Bronwen. Then he held off, realizing the danger of putting their opponent on the alert. He must conserve his energies for whatever struggle lay at the end of this journey.

'I thought we were done with all that foolishness,' grunted Hinde out of nowhere.

'Something more dangerous than foolishness.'

'Though who am I to talk of folly? I drove Elizabeth away. My boorishness . . .Whatever may have possessed her, I was the one who —'

'Mr. Hinde.' Caspian was in no mood for listening to maudlin self-pity. 'Mrs. Relph loves you. The real Mrs. Relph loves you and wants to marry you and wants above all to make you happy. Will you cling to that?'

'I don't know what right you have to — '

'You're always questioning people's qualifications. Just for once, sir, try to believe this for your own good. And for your sanity. Elizabeth will have need of your faith. Believe what you know to be true, and let's hope we come through. And that Elizabeth comes through, rather than the other.'

'The other?'

We shall see, thought Caspian grimly. He wondered who and what they would see.

Not a cosmic, cataclysmic force such as he and Bronwen had faced before, but one twisted self, battening on others. Did that make the conflict any less fearsome? One human mind, one consciousness, could be the burning-glass through which to concentrate all the evil in the universe.

* ★ ★

The woman came down the steps of the pulpit, Elizabeth watching her. Annie cowered against the end of a pew, edging backwards a few inches through the rustling paper she had been scattering about her.

'There's nothing to be scared of, Annie.'

The veil was thrown back over the shoulders like the hood of a cape. The long grey cloak was neutral; and neuter.

'I don't like it,' the girl moaned.

'It's what we've been promised, Annie.' Voice and features had reverted to being Wentworth. 'What I've been promising for both of us. So we can have a lifetime together.'

Bronwen stood her ground as the incongruously monkish figure approached. 'Mr. Wentworth, this other self you've invented — '

'Nothing is invented.'

'All your books,' she said. 'That's where you found Lilith and Theodora and the Countess and Ilona and all the others, isn't it? Don't you see the danger you're

341

in, Mr. Wentworth — danger from your own hallucinations.'

'You'll soon understand. She'll make you understand, as she has made us all understand.'

'You'll kill yourself.' He was close now, and she was frightened but furious — appalled at the grotesqueness that went hand in hand with obscenity and self-willed wickedness, the ugly absurdity, which made all evil a hundred times more awful. I despise you, she said silently into that sallow, gibbering face. I laugh at you — don't you hear me? 'Don't you realize that part of you is perversely planning your own death?'

She grabbed his arm.

She was set upon from behind. Claws fastened into her arms and dragged her aside. A kick in the ankle brought her down to the flagstones with a force that winded her. Annie was twisting her arm behind her back with a savagery learnt in the warlike streets where she had been bred.

'Just keep yer 'ands to yerself. Whatever he's doing, he knows what he's doing, so let him get on with it.'

'Don't damage her.' The voice shuddered between that of Wentworth and that of the deep-voiced woman. 'I shall need her unblemished.'

'Need her?' said Annie suspiciously.

Bronwen fought to get her breath back. How could another self, no matter how intensely its creator had come to believe in it, create such physical changes in the very flesh? Features shifted and distorted; the man's mouth curved into a woman's rapacious smile; eyes and eyelashes changed, age ebbed and flowed, two entities mingled and tugged apart.

Nursing her bruised elbow, Bronwen sat up. 'It's not going to succeed, Mr. Wentworth. The timetable's wrong. The elements won't combine. You've been misled into thinking I'm a Gemini subject.'

'I wasn't misled. Tell the lady what tomorrow is, Annie.'

Annie stared wonderingly into the molten features, obviously persuading herself it was just another of Wentworth's tricks, some clever game only he could play. 'It's my birthday,' she said.

'But — '

'You were the one to be misled, Mrs. Caspian. That's not what I chose you for.'

'Then for what?'

Bronwen knew she must play for time. The more protracted the ritual and the longer Wentworth and his dream psyche indulged in explanation and self-congratulation, the better the chance of Alexander reaching them and smashing the illusion. She longed to let her mind test his nearness. But whatever lurked within Wentworth's divided consciousness had already demonstrated some power of detecting their telepathic contacts: it had heard before, it might hear the resonance again.

'Mr. Wentworth,' she insisted, 'why have we been brought here?'

'I am Ilona.'

'That's one of your dreams, yes. The fantasy of Ilona — '

'I've tried so many relationships, Mrs. Caspian. I've been a woman who loved men, and a woman who loved women. Don't you envy me the fullness of my past? Then, thirty years ago, I picked out this young

344

man. Oh, yes, he was young when I chose him. I couldn't resist the experience of inhabiting the body of a man who loved boys. One must add all sensations to oneself if one's to appreciate the totality of existence. But this poor creature has not weathered too well. Ah, the inadequacy of ageing flesh, Mrs. Caspian.'

'Self-disgust,' said Bronwen. 'You've become disgusted with your own body, Mr. Wentworth, so you've had to invent another self and promise it youth and renewed vigour.'

'Recently I turned his tastes — *my* tastes — towards that girl. A slut, but a delicious slut. Most amusing.'

'You'll kill yourself. You'll kill both selves.'

'I am Ilona. I've lived untold lifetimes before and after Ilona, but hers is the self I'll not allow to die.'

The gowned figure moved away and lifted a copper bowl from a rack, which must once have held hymnbooks. She set it in the centre of the aisle and bowed low over it. Annie watched in fascination as the yellowed fingers unfolded a small sachet and tipped hair and nail parings into the bowl.

'Annie, will you come to me for a moment?'

Annie edged past Bronwen and searched the woman's face helplessly for someone else.

'Where *are* yer? Where've yer got to?'

'Hold out your left hand.' Annie extended a timorous hand, and with a quick snip of scissors the woman took a sliver of finger-nail. 'Now turn your head just a fraction.' Another snip, and a strand of hair was removed. 'And now will you scatter some more paper while I complete our prepara-tions? We shall want a good blaze in the centre — the sacred fire of consummation.'

Annie hesitated; but the note of command jogged her into obedience.

Ilona added the newly garnered hair and nail clippings to the bowl, and poured in oil from a small jar. She stirred the mixture unhurriedly with her little finger.

'As to the timetable being imperfect, Mrs. Caspian, I acknowledge your insight. I've rarely had ideal conditions for the reincarnation ceremony. Once I was left so weakened that I well-nigh brought about the death of the host body. But one strives for the closest approximation to the correct sequence.'

Bronwen got up and said, 'You are Edgar Wentworth, and nobody else. Become Wentworth again before you commit some suicidal blunder.'

'It's Wentworth who'll disappear, not I.' Ilona took a box of wax vestas from within the folds of her robe. 'You robbed me of Laura. Laura Hinde was to lodge me for the next twenty or thirty years — for as long as I could enjoy the use of her beauty. But she might have proved a problem at first, with such a puritanical upbringing to be overcome. I think I prefer the alternative which is now offered.'

She struck a match and lowered it into the bowl. Spirals of blue smoke curled thinly up and over the lip. One pungent waft stung in Bronwen's nostrils, and for a moment she was giddy, and in that same moment felt something just as pungent scrape across the surface of her mind as if testing it, seeking a spot through which to penetrate.

Annie had gone right to the end of the aisle to pull down more volumes and begin wrenching the pages from them.

Bronwen closed both hands over the door of Elizabeth's pew and shook it violently. It refused to open. She pulled herself forward, imploring: 'Wake, Elizabeth! Come back — come with me, wake up and she'll have no power over you. Come now!'

Elizabeth stared sightlessly past her.

Annie came running back up the aisle. 'What d'yer think yer up to?' The vindictive young face was thrust into hers.

Ilona had made no move. She stood above the bowl, inhaling the acrid incense. 'There's no call to be afraid, my dear Mrs. Caspian. Or perhaps I may start to call you Bronwen? We shall be on such familiar terms, soon.'

'You must open this door, and the outer door, and let us go: let Mrs. Relph and myself leave.'

'I'm afraid Mrs. Relph will not leave. But you will. Don't be afraid. You're not going to die.'

'Mr. Wentworth, will you listen to me . . .'

'You're the one who will walk out of here alive, when I'm ready. You robbed me of Laura, but I forgive you. We'll leave here unharmed,' said the throbbing, jubilant voice, 'when the ritual is complete: the two of us, you and I, in the same body.'

* * *

The gig swung up the slope, the mare whinnying at the last demand made on her. She stopped thankfully by the double gates, one of which was swinging open a few inches.

The two men jumped down, their footsteps and the heavy breathing of the horse the only sounds in the prim, self-sufficient street.

'What would they be doing in a place like this?' Hinde protested.

Caspian led the way up the path to the chapel.

He tried the heavy ring of the door handle. It turned, but the door was locked and would not open. There was no sound through the thick walls and woodwork. Could he possibly have guessed wrong?

Hinde walked impatiently along the north side of the building. 'Caspian, are you sure you know what . . . ' Then he looked up at one of the grimy windows. 'There's a fire — I'll swear there's a fire in there!'

Caspian hurried to his side. Undoubtedly there was a red glow from within, and the flicker of mounting flames on the inside of the dark panes.

'The fire brigade!' exclaimed Hinde.

'No time for that. Or for going and arguing a key out of Dingley.'

Caspian leaned against the brickwork and let his body go limp. His mind reached out. There was no longer time for concealment. He called to Bronwen; and heard the rush of her loving response.

'They're inside.'

He was in there with them. Through a ferment of drifting smoke and flame he felt Bronwen's dizziness, and saw a cloud of shifting shapes which would not stay in focus. Only Elizabeth Relph was quite still, quite aloof: waiting in a trance that went beyond mere human resignation.

He caught Bronwen's reeling mind and tried to steady it. And a voice resonated through and in the two of them: 'So you've arrived, Dr. Caspian. Welcome.'

Ilona stood erect at the west end of the aisle, with flames gathering height and ferocity about her. The red gleam in her feral eyes matched the tongues of fire, and she held out the smoking bowl at arms' length in unflinching oblation.

Caspian forced his whole self into the chapel and, linked soul and mind with Bronwen, forced Ilona's clouded outline to steady.

'Stay where you are, Dr. Caspian. We'll soon be with you. When I'm part of your wife she'll take the key from this dead husk, and we'll come to join you.'

Thought and speech and touch were all one. Annie's jumbled fears were a dissonance in his mind, and for a moment there was a flicker as if Wentworth had groped up from the depths for her, only to fall back; and there was Bronwen trying to make her limbs obey her, trying to raise a hand and strike the copper bowl from Ilona's grip. But minds and hands were trapped. They were drugged, entangled in a poisoned web. The miasma of Ilona's mind dripped narcotically over them. Bronwen felt the nauseous caress of it streaming over and stroking her mind, exploring with obscene fingers that left a slime all over her. Caspian pressed his brow to the wall, trying to restrain his fingers from scratching vainly at the bricks and mortar, concentrating his energies in one direction and one only. What between Bronwen and himself had been a shared, enriching sensuality was here a monstrous defilement.

Don't fight against me. Accept.

Wentworth. Caspian shouted it silently. *Come out. Don't yield. Come out before it's too late.*

Ilona's sleeves were ablaze, but Wentworth's tranced body felt nothing. There was smoke and the smell of smoke and the spell of what still curled up from the copper bowl; minds writhed in and out of one another; but there was only that obscene touch — no pain, no sense of the scorching fire.

Ilona began to walk slowly through the heart of the blaze.

The three of us will be two. An experience quite new to me. So delectable. The three of us two — while you two are already one.

Caspian and Bronwen fought back. *You'll not be admitted.*

But I'm already beginning to move in. You can feel it. We can feel it.

Bronwen winced, and even that instant of weakness slackened the bond between her and Caspian.

Ilona laughed. They did not hear the laugh, but felt it. *Your husband will never be sure whose mind he is likely to be communing with. Your husband — our husband. We shall play such exquisite games with him. Such new diversions. I have centuries of experience, there's so much we can learn together.*

She stopped by the pew in which Elizabeth was waiting.

Caspian and Bronwen reached out urgently for Elizabeth, and found it impossible to touch her. Her mind was locked away. For this, as for the door, only Ilona had the key.

Elizabeth, you must hear us, you must . . .

'Elizabeth!' It was a faint shout from the outside, impossibly distant world. Hinde was standing back and yelling up at the window. He caught Caspian's shoulder, pulling him away from the wall and away from Bronwen. 'We can't just stand here while the place burns down. Just propping yourself against the wall . . . '

'You fool! Let me get back to them.'

Caspian clutched at Bronwen's mind.

Ilona was standing with her hand outstretched towards Elizabeth. Flame ran like a will-o'-the-wisp down one sleeve and began to char the flesh of the open palm. The pair of scissors which had been used to collect the fragments of nail and hair glinted as Elizabeth took them.

'In the left breast,' intoned Ilona. 'In the heart. When I command.'

She'll feel no pain. A pity, in a way. Pain can add such potency.

'Come with me, Annie.'

The hand was extended again, blackening as fire consumed it and ran up inside

354

the sleeve. Wentworth's straggly hair about Ilona's rapt face was sputtering and smouldering.

Annie began to cry, and backed away.

'Let her go!' cried Bronwen aloud.

Their feet seemed to brace on solid ground, which would at any second be undermined. They held fast; and Ilona struggled to thrust past the barrier of their will.

'Annie!'

The girl clung to the edge of the nearest pew, but let go again and hastily pulled back her left foot as flame ran towards it over curling edges of paper.

Let go. Let her go.

Time was running out. For the first time they felt Ilona falter. The face crumpled. In a brief contortion of unstable flesh the ghost of Wentworth was allowed through.

'Annie' — it was the voice she knew, through the smoke she could believe it was the face she knew — 'you must trust me, you must come to me.'

Annie shuffled a reluctant step towards the flames.

Ilona willed Wentworth to draw her on. 'Elizabeth!'

There was a crash of breaking glass. Jagged pieces sprayed out over pews and the floor. Hinde, punching a wider hole with gloved hand, clutched the window frame with the other hand and blinked down into the smoke and fumes.

Ilona's mind shrieked through and over Wentworth's.

Flames sucked the draught in through the high gap in the window. Blazing sheets were spun up into a whirlpool. A shower of them singed Annie's neck and drove her uncontrollably towards the blazing figure of Wentworth. Ilona's face strove to reassert itself as Annie groped for her hands — hands beginning to blister and bubble.

'Now!' screeched Ilona. 'Elizabeth — the virgin blood — *now!*'

Hinde dropped heavily, narrowly missing the end of a bench, and pulled himself along into the aisle.

'You're mad! And you're wrong!' He could not take in what he saw, but he was gasping hysterically. 'It's not so. Elizabeth, you know it's not so . . . '

Caspian sprang up from outside the window, knees bent between his arms, and on into the chapel. He was hurled almost bodily aside by the fearsome blast of Ilona's hatred. She was struggling to hold him and Bronwen off while she grappled for supremacy over Annie and Elizabeth. But there was another self, rising up within her. Wentworth refused to be beaten down. Her voice was twisted; her face twisted and fought for survival. It became Wentworth's face — seared by agony as the man's consciousness surged back and awoke to the knowledge of devouring fire.

He screamed. But words howled through the scream.

'No, this isn't the promise . . . I've been cheated . . . not this. Annie, go back . . . you'll not have Annie, never, I'll never . . . '

'And you'll not have Elizabeth!' cried Bronwen, suddenly understanding, 'for she's no longer the virgin you chose.'

Hinde kicked blazing paper aside and began to kick the door of the pew until it

357

buckled and the catch sprang free. Elizabeth's eyes shut, then opened again. She swayed, looking wonderingly at him, and muttered sounds that made no sense yet meant everything.

'I'll not have Annie killed!' Wentworth, making one last great effort before Ilona engulfed him, threw the girl from him so that she reeled and spun away, jarring her shoulder and stumbling on past the pulpit.

Caspian sprang to Bronwen's side. The human torch spat fiery rage at them. Bronwen felt the alien being seeking a lodgment on her mind, desperately clutching, heaving itself over her, in spite of the unfulfilled ritual frenziedly struggling to survive as it wrapped itself round her and wailed to be let in. Wentworth's dying agonies were flailed down by Ilona's greed to live.

Their minds threw her back.

So many lives . . . so many more to live . . . I'll not die now, can't die now . . .

Caspian strode through the curling, blackening paper and held out his hand.

'The key.'

Ilona's mind flew like a demented moth in and out of their minds, beating her wings against their adamant denial.

Caspian snatched the key from fingers scorched to the bone, with no strength left to grip it. He tossed it to Bronwen and caught hold of the thing that was neither Wentworth nor Ilona now but only a pillar of smoking, reeking horror. He tried to pull it out of the flames but the flames came with it, and the fierceness of ultimate pain and despair in Bronwen's mind and Caspian's was such that they had to unclasp their grip — Caspian still holding the scarecrow arm but unable to cope with the pain of death as it keened up into brain and spirit.

Suddenly Ilona was gone; and Wentworth was gone. The two surrendered — Wentworth sobbing a last hideous rasp from a mouth too ravaged to frame syllables any more, Ilona making a last despairing flight off into oblivion.

'You'll be all right, everything will be all right,' Hinde was saying meaninglessly to Annie as he guided her to the door and waited for Bronwen to bring the key and open it.

Elizabeth leaned on him. Annie tugged away. Flame danced capriciously after them.

'You're safe.' Bronwen opened the door and they fled into the incredible ordinariness of daylight on a north London street.

'No.' Annie was battling, not against Hinde but against something within herself. She tried momentarily to turn back. 'He can't have gone, he can't have been taken, it's not . . . no, he . . . ' Then she was calm. She giggled unsteadily. 'No, he hasn't. There's something left.' She put a hand on her stomach and moaned as if she felt a twinge of pain there. 'Funny. Something tugging — and now it's gone . . . '

She began to weep. Hinde led her and Elizabeth on to the parched grass. And suddenly Annie broke free, and raced down the path to the gate.

Flame licked out of the shattered window.

Within, the burning carcass that was beyond saving fell at Caspian's feet. He

360

stepped back, burns staining his wrists. Fire died from the body because there was so little left to consume.

Only a vestige of a face remained in a hellish grimace: Ilona's face dissolving through age and decay and wickedness, loosening its grip, dying away into embers until it left only a charred yet strangely peaceful caricature of Edgar Wentworth.

15

The moon silvered the cupola of the little temple folly and picked out a few pale gleams from the shadowy colonnade. Looking past her husband's shoulder, through the drawing room window, Bronwen was soothed by the cool formality of the landscape after the blazing furies of the day. But she wondered whether, had Nasmyth Lodge been their home, she and Caspian would ever have been able to dismiss the memory of the creature which, driven from the house as Edgar Wentworth, hid in that temple as Ilona, waiting to spring. Hinde would be undisturbed by such recollections. He had not sensed the presence there, and would continue refusing to attribute his brother-in-law's behaviour that night to anything other than drunkenness.

In time, too, he would doubtless find a cosily rational explanation for what he had witnessed this afternoon.

They had reported the fire, handed

Wentworth's remains into the keeping of the local infirmary, and made a statement to the police: a statement as bare and noncommittal as Hinde, in his position in the public eye, could have wished.

'And the whole truth,' said Caspian, gingerly crossing his bandaged wrists, 'can be confided to Priestley at Scotland Yard. I think we owe it him.'

'Not that he'll believe you,' said Bronwen.

They heard Hinde's footsteps in the hall. He had been upstairs making sure that Elizabeth was comfortably settled and that Laura could sit with her. Now, entering the room, he must have caught the end of their conversation.

'Don't blame the fellow if he doesn't believe a word of it. In fact, he's not up to his job if he does believe it.' He let himself subside into a chair between the two of them. 'It's enough to make one propose an Act of Parliament for restoration of the witchcraft laws.'

'Elizabeth's not too badly shaken?' asked Bronwen.

'She seems to have come to no harm,

thank God. At the moment she remembers less than we do, though she was in the thick of it. I take it there's no necessity for reminding her?'

'If we told her the details,' said Caspian, 'they'd mean virtually nothing. She wouldn't relate any of them to her waking awareness. And the deeper experiences won't be reawakened: there's nobody now with any hold on her. The spell has been broken.'

'That evil rogue — what was his name? — Wentworth. I was right about him and his kind from the start. But what in heaven's name he hoped to achieve with all that foul mumbo-jumbo about virgin blood and . . . and . . . ' He shrugged it away with loathing.

Bronwen glanced at Caspian.

He said carefully: 'The thing that possessed Wentworth believed in ritual, in sacrifice and in the efficacy of alchemy. Not in an actual physical elixir of life, but in the psychic transmutation of other lives into immortality. Instead of a magic potion there was to be a mesmeric transference at death. Originally it was planned that the reincarnation should be from Wentworth's body to your daughter's; then, when Laura had been effectively shielded and, as it were, treated with an antidote, it was to be from Wentworth's body to my wife's.'

'It's inconceivable.'

'The human mind conceives many things. But — in this case the conviction faltered towards the end. Or Wentworth's own love for that girl was stronger than the underlying purpose of the ritual.'

'You call that love? A seedy, ageing lecher's infatuation with a little gutter-snipe . . .'

'His infatuation was at all events strong enough to defeat Ilona.'

'Would it have succeeded,' pondered Bronwen, 'if all the elements had been assembled in the correct sequence, each under its ideal aspect, instead of her adjusting the available material to suit her own impatience — and being subconsciously aware that she was compromising?'

'Adjusting things,' growled Hinde, 'to suit his own fiction. *His*,' he insisted. He would not pay even lip service to this baffling concept of Ilona.

'And that fiction,' said Caspian, 'demanded the shedding of virgin blood in the final psychic elixir. She had chosen Elizabeth as the virgin sacrifice, but could not have known that since making the choice and indoctrinating her, there had been a change.'

Hinde reddened. 'That outburst of mine in the chapel,' he said gruffly. 'Wasn't aware what I was saying. Can't think how I could have blurted it out — '

'You blurted it out because you felt intuitively what those circumstances demanded. Whatever you feel now, you sensed the truth then. And it may be that your revelation was the blow that finally broke Ilona's strength. According to her ritual, the vital ultimate ingredient had been rendered powerless. In those last moments, when she was raging about our minds, she tried to overcome the loss by sheer force of will. But her own belief had been destroyed. You, more than anyone, saved Elizabeth.'

Hinde looked gratified; but uncomprehending.

It was simpler, in spite of the lingering exhaustion of the recent conflict, for

Caspian and Bronwen to commune silently. They could see the pattern of events as Hinde would never be persuaded to see it.

Ilona had chosen the most susceptible candidates from those who answered her original advertisement and attended her first meetings. Perhaps right at the start she had been forced to make certain compromises. Among those discarded were some whose birth dates and prevailing influences fitted her psychic equation, but who would not readily submit to her influence. She had to use those most malleable. The ideal sequence would have begun with the death of Elaine Mancroft as the earth subject, followed by Thornhill's air element; then a water figure between him and the final contribution of fire. But Ilona had chosen Henry Garston, born under Pisces, as the earlier water subject, most probably by reason of his willingness to co-operate — his impatience, even, to surrender himself.

The one element that could not be manoeuvred out of place was that of fire.

They had been mistaken to associate Laura Hinde with it: that had never been her appointed role. It had been left until the end because Wentworth himself was a Leo subject, under the rule of fire, and his body could not be offered for annihilation until everything else had been accomplished.

I wouldn't be surprised, Caspian confided, *to find if we consult the relevant ephemeris that, although we're still not in the actual Leo period, the conjunctions of its most powerful influences, the Sun and Neptune, are as favourable today as at any time between the birth degrees. That's why today was decreed rather than some date after the 23rd of July, when some of the power of the other elements might have waned.*

They thought of the obscene whirlpool into which their minds had been churned; and marvelled at the stillness after the storm.

If she had not lost Laura and Thornhill, and not tried makeshift substitutes at the last moment, would her conviction not have wavered but carried her through?

'Do you suppose,' said Bronwen aloud,

wanting to break that fraught silence, 'that she's really dead and there's absolutely no trace left?'

Hinde shifted uneasily. 'I'm sure we're all very tired. I think we ought to agree on a consistent, straightforward story for your police friend. The truth, of course — nothing but the facts — but playing down the more extreme aspects of Wentworth's abduction of Mrs. Relph.'

Caspian, answering the question which really mattered, said to Bronwen: 'Perhaps some trace of that personality will vibrate on the air somewhere, waiting to strike a chord in someone receptive. Waiting to be brought back to life by the Aeolian harp of another mind, its strings tuned to the same resonance.'

★　★　★

Annie knew where the keys of the till and of the safe were kept. She opened them both and found herself eighty-two pounds better off. And better that she should have the money — she was sure he'd have wanted her to take it — than for it to be left for whoever came and found clever legal excuses for claiming the place and its contents.

Then there were her clothes. He had bought her a few fancy things, though after her first excitement she hadn't worn them much. One dress with a smart bustle had suited her very well when they walked out together; but that was something they had rarely done. Mr. Wentworth had preferred his pleasures indoors. Now she took it down, held it against herself in front of the mirror, and decided to put it on.

She didn't want to fill a case and have to carry it through the streets. She had no idea where she was going, and she wasn't anxious to be accused, this very night or later, of stealing from a dead man's home.

Dead. Tears came to her eyes as she thought of it. Just because one of those mad games of his had got out of hand. It wasn't fair. He had been a toff in his way, in spite of those funny ideas. Not that she minded *those*. She would miss him. There were lots of things she would miss.

Or would she? Did she need to?

Something stirred in her mind: something strange, like a secret voice of her own which she'd never listened to before. It was very faint — nothing you could actually have an argument with, or even hear quite clearly. But it struck up a provoking little tune which, now she came to think of it, had chased her when she ran from the chapel and those people who would have meant her no good, and somehow clung to her like a moth caught in her hair, in danger of letting go yet managing to keep a grip. It fluttered weakly there while she was getting ready to leave the shop, and was with her still as she slammed the door behind her and walked off with the money in her reticule and her new feather boa round her neck.

'What'll become of me?'

The question made her laugh, though she didn't know why, as she walked down the dark alley and out into the lights, turning towards the even brighter lights which beckoned from Regent Street and the Haymarket.

She quickened her pace and was almost running, as she used to run when

371

someone was after her, or as she had run from the hellfire of the chapel. Then she slowed to an adult, enticing, knowledge-able walk.

Somehow, something was telling her that she was going to do very nicely for herself.

THE END

We do hope that you have enjoyed reading this large print book.

Did you know that all of our titles are available for purchase?

We publish a wide range of high quality large print books including:
Romances, Mysteries, Classics
General Fiction
Non Fiction and Westerns

Special interest titles available in large print are:
The Little Oxford Dictionary
Music Book, Song Book
Hymn Book, Service Book

Also available from us courtesy of Oxford University Press:
Young Readers' Dictionary
(large print edition)
Young Readers' Thesaurus
(large print edition)

For further information or a free brochure, please contact us at:
Ulverscroft Large Print Books Ltd.,
The Green, Bradgate Road, Anstey,
Leicester, LE7 7FU, England.
Tel: (00 44) 0116 236 4325
Fax: (00 44) 0116 234 0205

THE CAPTIVE CLAIRVOYANT

Brian Ball

The Baker Street Irregulars, the gang of ragamuffins who sometimes assist Sherlock Holmes in his investigations, put their wits and courage to the test against kidnapping, robbery and murder . . . A boy announces that he has seen a ghost, but the truth is far more terrifying . . . A gypsy seeks vengeance from beyond the grave . . . An ancient evil awakens and desires fresh victims . . . These five stories of mystery, horror and the occult from the pen of Brian Ball will thrill and chill in equal measure.

THE ASH MURDERS & OTHER STORIES

Edmund Glasby

An apparent case of spontaneous human combustion is enough to test the very limits of Detective Inspector Dryer's beliefs, so when Augustus Smith appears, claiming that the victim was targeted by an ancient demon and that others will suffer the same fate, this proves too much to take. But could Smith possibly be telling the truth . . . ? This and four other tales of the strange and mysterious make up this collection from Edmund Glasby.

THE PRIVATE EYE

Ernest Dudley

Nat Craig, London's foremost private investigator, believes in hitting first and pulling no punches, which makes for exciting episodes, including murder, blackmail and robbery, from his case-book. The indomitable Craig ruthlessly tracks down the evil-doer, and each case contains a genuine and logical problem of detection . . .

SHERLOCK HOLMES TAKES A HAND

Vernon Mealor

An exciting trio of tales following the escapades of Colonel Sebastian Moran, 'one of the best shots in the world' and the 'second most dangerous man in London', according to Sherlock Holmes. Find out how Moran achieves his position at the right hand of Professor Moriarty in 'The Hurlstone Selection'; shares lodgings with Holmes, Watson, and Mrs Hudson in 'The Man with the Square-Toed Boots'; and turns his skills to art theft in 'The Disappearance of Lord Lexingham'.